C000293927

PRAISE FOR THE

"The stories that form Prabda [~~Yoon's~~] [~~mind-bending~~] [~~and~~] strangely melancholic universe are unfailingly provocative... Playful, coolly surrealist... this landmark collection... is not only the first of Yoon's work to be translated into English, but a rare international publication of Thai fiction... Mui Poopoksakul's translation renders the stories fluent and accessible, ironing out the linguistic kinks and allowing Yoon's portraits of Bangkok lives to take centre stage." — *Financial Times*

"Evocative, erudite, and often very funny stories of Bangkok life." — *The Guardian*

"Very, very clever... A completely fabulous book."
— *Monocle 24: Meet the Writers*

"*The Sad Part Was* is unique in the contemporary literature of Bangkok—it doesn't feature bar girls, white men, gangsters or scenes redolent of *The Hangover Part II*. Instead it reveals, sotto voce, the Thai voices that are swept up in their own city's wild confusion and energy, and it does so obliquely, by a technique of partial revelation always susceptible to tenderness." — *New Statesman*

"Young prodigy Yoon's style seems most influenced by the street-smart, chatty American posse, and revels in all kinds of contemporary twists of the postmodern and meta kind. However its savviness never tips into the sort of self-congratulatory indulgence that many of its western peers suffer from, and it remains charming throughout."
— *The Big Issue*

MOVING
PARTS

TRANSLATED BY

MOVING PARTS

PRABDA YOON

MUI POOPOKSAKUL

TILTED AXIS PRESS

ร่าง rang

---

noun. body, shape, form, figure
verb. to draft, to sketch

The Thai word leaves open two possibilities: the body
as both a mere rough sketch of the self and at the
same time its foundation. The stories in this collection
explore these interlocking aspects of our physicality.

PART 1: YUCKING FINGER

"You have one chance to redeem yourself, Maekee." Ms. Wonchavee's voice seeped through every fiber of the eleven-year-old's nerves.

And it even ran to the tip of his tongue, giving the boy with a buzz cut enough of a flavor to know: his teacher's voice tasted bitter.

Maekee ("His papa's name's Maeka. Hahahaha. Maeka came to see Maekee, Teacher lashed them in the heinie, both Maekee and Maeka. Hahahaha.") pursed his lips so hard that blood was wrung up to the apples of his cheeks. The chalk in his right hand, which hovered over the blackboard, was trembling. He felt trouble brewing in his tummy, and closer to the tail end of that situation—there was no question about it—the area already felt oddly distended, dragging and distressing, as though within seconds the orbs of his butt cheeks were going to blow into pieces.

X to the third power plus Y to the third power

equals one hundred fifty-two.

Comma.

X squared Y plus X Y squared equals one hundred twenty.

English letters, numbers, mathematical symbols— these things were ganging up on him with their glares of derision.

Young Maekee's task was to find the value of X.

Why on earth do you have to find it? Just let X be X. Why is it that when you come across an X, you have to insist on knowing what number it really signifies? Maybe it doesn't appreciate being an object of public attention.

"Hurry up, Maekee. Your stalling is wasting your classmates' valuable learning time."

("Maek's a dumb nickname, being called Cloud is lame, his father is to blame. Hahahaha.")

With a right-handed grip, the boy landed the white, powdery stick on the blackboard. Confusion was blooming and even bearing fruit inside his skull. Everything he had ever learned seemed in that moment to have been snatched up by panic and shuffled and stirred together until chunks of information practically ricocheted off one another inside the two halves of his brain.

Last night I dreamed about a crab... The crab

was crawling along the beach. When I grabbed it and sniffed it, it pinched my nose with its right claw. Shocked, I screamed in pain, ouch! And then I hurled the crab into the ocean. It was really angry at me. It refused to be defeated and hurried off to fetch its mother from her hole. The mother was very large, even larger than me. On top of that, she had a human head and looked exactly like my mother. But the crab called her, mother, mother, therefore the mother crab probably wasn't my mother. The little crab, that tattletale, told its mother that I'd attacked it. I shot back that the little crab attacked me first, but at the end of the day, a mother's always going to side with her offspring, so the mother crab chose to believe the little crab over me. This being the case, she scowled and threatened to pinch my neck clean through. I tried to negotiate. I said, can't you pinch some other part? I have a sore throat. But the mother crab didn't listen and insisted on cutting my throat, so I had to run away. I didn't get far before I heard my own mother call me:

"Maek, Maek, wake up, sweetie. Otherwise you're not going to make it to school in time for the national anthem."

I startled awake, saw that my clock said it was 7:15. Oh no, I'd got up late again. And I hadn't finished my homework. I still had three questions left.

I bolted into the bathroom, did my business as fast as possible, and then went into the kitchen to look for something to eat. My mother was sitting there pounding some kind of chili paste. I looked up at the clock on the wall. Oh! It was only 6:50... or had I showered back in time? I ran back to look at the clock on my bedside table. It turned out the short hand was still at seven and the long hand at three—it was still 7:15 just like it was earlier. That meant my clock wasn't working, so I felt a little relieved.

But not very relieved, because, in any case, my homework wasn't done. And I didn't know how to do it. That was why I hadn't finished it in the first place. I have no stomach for Xs and Ys. My mother thought I would be late for school if I took the bus, so she asked Aunt Louie from next door if she could drop me off. I couldn't complain—I like riding in the back of Aunt Louie's motorbike. It's nice and cool, even if the pollution smells bad. Aunt Louie's nice, too. And her body's squishy—it's kind of fun to hold on to. She asked me if I'd finished my homework. I fibbed and said yes. A Buddhist precept broken again, always the same one. But what was I supposed do? It's what they call a white lie—it doesn't hurt anybody. When I got to school and ran into Muay, she immediately started running her mouth, making fun of me.

"Maeka came to see Maekee, Teacher lashed them in the heinie, both Maeka and Maekee. Hahahaha."

Yeah, yeah, laugh.

I asked Piag if I could copy his homework but he wouldn't let me. Piag's a prig—he thinks he's Ms. Wonchavee's favorite. So I ended up having to make up the answers. As it turned out, they were all wrong. When it was time for Ms. Wonchavee's class, she asked, "Are you the only dumb one in this class, huh, Maekee? When you're in class, do you pay attention? Come here. Come to the front of the class, and let's see you solve this problem." Then she went about writing an equation on the blackboard. I couldn't even get my saliva down when I saw the problem— how was I supposed to solve it?

"Now, are you going to make me wait until you're old enough to have facial hair?" Ms. Wonchavee snapped.

Some of my classmates were snickering through their teeth ("Maekee got spanked, Maekee got kicked. Maeka got tanked and kicked Maekee. Hahaha."), but they froze as soon as they caught Ms. Wonchavee's roving eyes of fury.

"Whoever finds this funny will get to suck on a real bitter chunk of giloy," she promised.

Maekee gulped and then pressed the tip of the chalk on the board and started dragging it.

He took a while scratching shapes out of white powder. Once he was through, what could be read was: X equals one, comma, two.

Maekee thought he was hearing things when he heard a little voice emanating from his finger.

"Yuck."

The classroom was completely silent. Ms. Wonchavee approached the boy at the blackboard, who was shivering as if he had fever chills.

"Do you think this is the right answer?" she asked in a frosty tone. Instead of acknowledging the question with a verbal reply, Maekee shook his head. "Are you mute, Maekee?" He shook his head again. "There you go, shaking your head again. If this isn't being mute, then what do you call it? Tell me."

This time the boy kept his head down and still, not knowing what words to utter.

"Answer me," Ms. Wonchavee pressed.

"I'm not mute, ma'am." It cost him a great deal of effort to get the sentence unstuck from the roof of his mouth.

"So, if you're not mute, tell me if what you have on the blackboard is the correct answer?"

"No, ma'am." ("Have you finished your homework, Maekee?" "Yes, I already finished it last night.")

"I gave you a chance to redeem yourself, and you still can't get it right. What does this mean? Explain it to me. Tell me the reason. Why?"

"I don't know how to do it, ma'am." His lips blanched.

Maekee got smacked on the palms with a metal ruler, five times on each hand. ("Count it! Louder!")

Having received his punishment, Maekee returned to sit at his desk. Although his hands still throbbed from the itchy sting, he'd already put the anxiety, the agony and the embarrassment suffered in front of the blackboard out of his mind.

Then he remembered the strange sound he'd heard, the one that'd leaked out from the tip of his finger.

He put all five fingers of his right hand in front of his face.

Thumb, index finger, middle finger, ring finger, pinky. All five constituents appeared normal.

I must have been hearing things. What kind of finger can make sounds?

Maekee's assigned desk was situated by the window. What he saw when he looked outside were two large tamarind trees that spread their branches and leaves over a patch of the parking lot.

For several semesters now, he'd used details of the two tamarind trees as resting points for his eyes. They were like air-framed pictures that served as wellsprings of imagination. Whenever he looked out, Maekee didn't simply see two trees; sometimes he saw monsters, sometimes he saw superheroes, sometimes he saw the face of a certain young lady named Noon (a student in fifth grade, homeroom two, at whom he'd been stealing glances at every opportunity), sometimes he looked out because he wanted to see nothing at all.

Ms. Wonchavee resumed her lesson plan ("Today we're starting a new chapter. There will be no permission granted to go do any kind of business. Whoever has to go, number one or two, must hold it.")

As soon as the soundwaves carrying her voice hit Maekee's ears, he felt as if his yawning reflex had been triggered. His eyelids wanted to sink, his hand wanted to lift up and act as a pillow for his head.

To relieve his drowsiness, Maekee turned toward the window. A light breeze was blowing through the tamarind branches, gently ruffling them.

All of a sudden, his nostrils felt itchy, so he put his right hand in front of his face and wiggled the pinky deep into one of his breathing holes.

When it re-emerged in the outside world, the

retracted finger didn't show up empty-handed but bore a souvenir in the form of a crusty, dark-green nugget.

"Yuck."

This time Maekee was certain that his finger had cried "yuck."

That was the day Maekee became acquainted with his yucking finger. To this day, having been familiar with the sound for the better part of his life, he still wasn't sure which finger it was on his right hand that was the culprit. The thought had crossed his mind that it was the pointer finger, for the sole reason that its name indicated it might be inclined to make a point and state its opinion, but he'd never had any clear proof.

From that moment on, whatever Maekee held or touched appeared to be a source of dissatisfaction for the yucking finger, particularly if the situation involved an important matter in his life. He could trace it back to the instant he held a pencil in his hand while he took his secondary school entrance exam. When he finished the test, the finger made itself heard.

Maekee's initial theory was that the finger cried "yuck" when it felt that it was partaking in something that would lead his life down a path of failure. But as he grew more familiar with the workings of the yucking finger, he discerned that the key factor in its decision to make noise was, rather, dissatisfaction. As a matter of fact, it had assumed the role of his harshest personal critic.

It'd cried "yuck" when he finished his exam not because it thought he wasn't going to pass but merely because it didn't approve of the institution he wanted to attend. It'd cried "yuck" when Maekee located his name as he ran his finger over the list of success-ful university entrance exam takers, because it didn't agree with his choice to enroll in the architecture fac-ulty. When he and the then–Miss Piyawon held hands for the first time, the finger cried "yuck" because it felt the two weren't a sufficiently good match.

It used to cry "yuck" when he composed love let-ters to the aforementioned Piyawon. It said "yuck" every time he stroked her face lovingly. On their wedding day, the groom heard nothing but "yuck, yuck, yuck, yuck, yuck," hounding him for almost twenty-four hours.

Maekee worked as an architect, the profession he had always set his heart on ("yuck"). The house into which he and his wife moved and where they shared a life, he'd designed it with his own hands, every line and every corner of it ("yuck").

Maekee's decision to take up married life seemed

to have been the pivotal step that set the yucking finger off, and it huffed and puffed into a mental state that
qualified as lunacy. Its attacks became emotion-driven
criticism and out-of-line sarcasm. Maekee would tilt a
beer glass for a sip, and there'd be a "yuck." He'd hand
over money to pay for fried bananas, and there'd be a
"yuck." He'd press the button to call an elevator, and
there'd be a "yuck." He'd flip from Channel Seven to
Channel Five, and there'd be a "yuck." He'd roll down
the car window for some cool air, and there'd be a
"yuck." He'd withdraw money from an ATM to buy
groceries, and there'd be a "yuck." He'd hit a shuttle-
cock over the net to victory, and there'd be a "yuck."
He'd shake hands with an important client to greet
them, and there'd be a "yuck." He'd drop a one-baht
coin into the bowl of a sidewalk beggar, and there'd
be a "yuck."

Whenever he'd bend his wrist and point at his
own chest, the finger would cry, "yuck, yuck, yuck,
yuck, yuck, yuck."

"If you're not happy with what I do, then go
inhabit someone else's body!" Maekee yelled at his
own right hand, having reached his limits.

No one else ever heard the "yuck" from his hand.
Once, he'd tried to introduce the yucking finger
to Piyawon. ("It's quite a big part of my life, Won.

Even though I detest it to the bones, it refuses to go away. It's at the heart of why I've never felt certain about any decision I've ever made in life. It kills my self-confidence. Imagine this, Won. No matter what I touch, it starts going, 'yuck, yuck.' Yuck, Won—the sound of dissatisfaction, of disgust, of disapproval—with just about every step I take in life. I'm stuck with it. I've thought about cutting off all my fingers once and for all, but I couldn't do it. I couldn't bear going through with it. All of a sudden—to become a person with a stump for a hand—I couldn't cope with the idea. It even mocked me then, because I didn't have the guts to get rid of it. It started going, 'yuck, yuck,' even louder than usual. So I've learned to live with it instead. I've had to train myself to turn a blind eye to it since it's already a part of me. That's why, Won, I wanted you to meet it. Here, it's on my right hand here. Hey, make your yucking noise for Won. Do it, you! Do it! I told you to do it. How is it that on our first night in bed together, you were screaming in a fit all throughout our love-making? Oh, I forgot to tell you. It doesn't like you very much, Won—it's been saying 'yuck' since we first started dating.") His wife sat frozen, the disbelief in her ears showing in her eyes.

In that instant, Piyawon's mind started searching

for a new path for her life.

Without her having an inkling, as of yet, of the new life that was going to look for a path out of her belly.

—

The sky was bright and sunny this morning—why then, this afternoon, were the clouds dense and heavy as they dumped water down on the city?

Maekwon, whose nickname was Noom, was annoyed as she sat in her white car, observing the chaos from behind the windshield. The wipers were on medium speed, clearing the way for her eyes with their steady swings so she didn't have much trouble seeing the scene outside despite the thick curtain of water.

Turning to her right, Noom saw a soggy bunch of city dwellers of various sexes and ages, trying to huddle and squeeze together under the shelter of a bus stop. Some guarded their hairdos with their palms; some had adapted sheets of daily newspapers for use as shields against splashes. The lucky ones who had umbrellas had to share them by default with the strangers next to them, who got to lean on, or under, the former's good fortune.

The temperature in the car was already cool from

the air-conditioning, but the dreary, drippy weather outside lowered it by several degrees more. In unison, the pores along Noom's body prickled, prompting the fine hairs to stand on edge. Noom gripped the steering wheel tight as if ready at any moment to gun the car to the finish line. But traffic conditions were not cooperating at all: every car on the road had been at a standstill for a good hour.

Noom peeked at the watch on her left wrist. The time was 2:47 in the afternoon, according to its digital numbers.

Her eyes then turned to the mini-clock that came preinstalled in the car: the short hand was at the number two, and the long hand was at around forty-two. When she switched her gaze again to the radio display, the green numbers there said the current time was 2:45 p.m.

In a single location, Noom had three different times to choose to believe.

Regardless of which display she trusted, she was certain that the true time in terms of her life in that present moment—on this earth, in Thailand, in Bangkok, on Silom Road, in the white car, in the flesh-toned short-sleeved silk blouse and black pants, in the brown woven-leather shoes, in the navy-blue lace bra and underwear—would probably always elude her.

Even the division of the day into two halves doesn't offer certainty. Who says the sun inhabits the day and the moon the night? When Noom woke up this morning, the moon was still dangling out in the open, a faint trace in the sky, brazenly fraternizing with the sun. This sort of thing, the sun never does. He doesn't get carried away by the winds of his mood, lingering around into the hours of darkness. He rises and then he sets, steadfast in the performance of his duties since ancient times, unlike she of the creamy complexion, who sometimes shows up whole, sometimes half, sometimes crescent, sometimes not at all, her fickle and fitful nature inducing the tides to wax and wane along with her.

Noom had heard an astronomy theory (her son had read it to her) that the moon might have once been part of the earth, and then one fine day an unhumorously humongous meteorite from somewhere ran the red light, slamming blindly into our own heavenly body in an unheavenly manner. That astronomical force of collision caused a part of the earth's mass to break off and bounce out of its gravitational field, with the piece then being left to drift on the outside, eventually becoming a minion in the earth's orbit.

The sky over Bangkok right now was dark and dismal, with heavy clouds and a widespread storm. Nothing of the moon was visible, not even a sliver. Even the sun was struggling, nearly buried behind the curtain of black despite having been sitting out in the morning, happily shining its rays.

Regardless of what the actual time was, regardless of whether the moon used to be a part of the earth, Noom wanted merely to get to the hospital as soon as possible, before Maekee had taken his final breath.

She did not wish to accrue another memory.

Good or bad, a memory was an image of the past.

A sage once said, "Be present."

But for Noom, the present involved getting stuck in traffic, which somewhat dimmed the appeal of being there.

The water pouring down from the sky appeared to be getting thicker and thicker: it had turned from sprinkles into streams and now into a cascading wall of rain. The people who had to idle around under some sort of cover along the roadside were faced with a more serious predicament by the minute. Many started running at full steam to seek some immovable property that would keep them dry, so the population exposed to the elements was becoming sparser, with no one daring to stand their ground or challenge the storm any longer.

Noom was still clutching the steering wheel with both hands. Her mind—anxious—crossed dimensions and jumped ahead of real time. She saw an image of Maekee lying still on a white bed, hooked up to an IV at the arm, his eyes closed, his lips sealed, the beating in his chest feeble and drawn out.

With traffic still in a gridlock, those on the road looked agitated. Hundreds of pairs of eyebrows were knitted; if these could be knotted together, they could probably form a long braid.

Apart from the sound of Noom's breath, the hum of the air-conditioning, the noise of the engine, and the raindrop splats that slipped in from outside, the interior of the car was serenely quiet.

For Noom, Maekee had always been Maekee. When she'd been in situations where she had to call him by name, she addressed him as Khun Maekee, or sometimes Khun Maek, depending on the environment. Never once had the word "Father" slipped out of her mouth. The responsibilities that came with that word should involve more than giving biological seed. Since Noom felt this way, her calculation of the word had never produced Maekee as the result. She already had a father; his name was Pipop. Even though it wasn't his seed that was the source of her life, Papa

Pipop had performed every inch of the duties that summed up the word almost perfectly. Why would she need two fathers?

But today Maekee was dying.

Even though she didn't consider him her father, some string of attachment made her want to see the old man's face one last time (the eleventh time in her life).

A chill was spreading through her hands while traffic showed no sign of moving.

She cast a glance at the air-conditioning controls on the black dashboard, and, after a few seconds' deliberation, freed her left hand from the steering wheel and twisted the knob to turn the AC down.

"Yuck," her finger cried.

—

"Hello, yes, yes, Maekee speaking. What was that? Really? When did she give birth? A girl! Really? Is she cute? A-ha. All's fine? A-ha. I'm coming right now. That's okay. A-ha. Thank you, bye. Ha! I have a kid! It's a girl, too. A daughter. Can you guys help cover for me for a bit? I'm going to the hospital. I have to go see my baby's face. I have a kid! I'll hurry back and deal with all this again immediately—don't worry. I'm off. Yeah, thanks, thanks."

"To Chula Hospital please. Yeah, I'm alright. I'm just excited—my ex-wife just gave birth. My first child ever. Ex, yes, ex—she broke up with me. It's a long story. Please drive faster. I'm dying to see the baby's face."

"Room 503. Thank you. I'm the baby's father."

"Hello Father. Won's already awake?"

"Hi Won. How are you feeling? Are you still in pain? Oh, where is she? Can I see our baby girl?"

"Won! Won! I'm holding this child. Will you be my witness? I'm using both hands to cradle my own daughter. Right? Do you see this, Won? Every one of my fingers is touching the child! They're really making physical contact with her. Won, look, they are, right? It's not making any noise, Won, my finger's not making any noise. The yucking finger's not yucking anymore! It probably likes our baby. It's not putting me down anymore. Won, listen—there's no more 'yuck'!"

Piyawon looked alarmed. She tried to snatch the newborn from Maekee's embrace as he filled the room with his uproar.

Piyawon's father jumped in to provide reinforcement.

"What's gotten into you, Maekee? Let go of the child."

The commotion reached the doctors and nurses' ears.

A moment later in Room 503, a small-scale riot broke out between Maekee and everyone else in the world.

In the end, the baby was reclaimed and safely returned to her mother's side.

Maekee sank to the floor, tears streaming out of his eyes.

"What did I do wrong? Can't I be happy that my finger accepts this important thing in my life? None of you understands the disparagement I've had to bear." "Let me hold my daughter a bit longer. At least I'm her father. I'm the father!"

With his right hand, Maekee pointed at himself.

"Yuck."

PART 2: EVIL TONGUE

"Murderer" is not what I wish to call myself, the main reason being that it isn't my name.

But what that is, is inconsequential. Even if I were to tell you my name, you'd be bound to call me "murderer" anyway.

Some titles, it's so easy to make them stick. You execute a single deed, it becomes a big story, and you have the title officially bestowed on you instantly. My whole life, I've gone to bed every night and woken up every day, and yet no one has proclaimed me a sleeper or a waker. Every morning I used to leave for work, carried by the muscles of my legs and feet, and yet no one has hailed me a walker.

You take one person's life, and you're a fully decorated murderer!

I hadn't had a chance to hone my skills, to garner the experience of a seasoned murderer, to taste the gaminess of blood the way professionals do, to

call somebody else "victim" in a full-throated manner, and I was already as much a murderer as any of
my neighbors in the adjacent cells. In the eyes of the
public, once the label "murderer" is in play, the per-
petrators tend to be viewed as having roughly the
same skill level, no matter how many guns they've
wagged, how many bodies they've put underground,
how many heads they've bagged, how many hands
they've bound, how many mouths they've gagged,
how many lives they've downed.

Murderer... it's easy to be one, but hard to start.

I myself had waited some twenty years before I
felt ready, body and mind, to carry out the vital deed
that day.

Although I'm not particularly fond of my new title,
I'm not the least bit troubled by my being a murderer
for one reason: at least you're not here to witness the
fact, Mother. At least I don't have to worry about
how to explain it to you. I probably wouldn't lie to
the woman who bore me, probably wouldn't come
up with tales to deceive you and make you believe
that I'm innocent.

You would probably be quite devastated over the
ill fate of your only remaining child. You probably
wouldn't be able to bear the sight of the shabby cage
in which your dear son is confined. You would prob-

ably lose sleep, sobbing your eyes out at night until your tears run red from heartbreak and from the pity you feel for your flesh and blood, who has turned into a tumor of society, into a filthy scum that nobody wants to associate with any longer.

I myself couldn't fathom, and I don't even dare imagine, the magnitude of the emotional trauma that the events which took place would likely inflict on you. I know only that you would be much saddened, and the word "much" here is one that carries more meaning than the normal "much;" it's a "much" at a level beyond the reach of language. How much sadder would you be if you knew that person whose breath your dear son put out with his own hands is... you yourself, Mother.

Day___ Month___ Year___

Dear Mother,

The prison cell is rather dirty, but it's not quite so filthy as to be unbearable. There is some air circulation. You don't have to worry about my allergies acting up—there's no sign of any symptoms so far. People in here are personable for the most part. They have a habit of cursing, but that's to be expected. They aren't educated people like we are. But no one has plainly presented himself as my enemy. There's a bit of teasing and sarcasm; I've never taken the nonsense to heart.

I often get asked, how could I do it, how did I have the heart to kill my mother and on top of it butcher her soulless body into tiny little pieces? Didn't I feel anything? Didn't I fret at all over the colossal sin that would shove me into a freefall toward the lowest pits of hell and preclude any possibility of reincarnation for hundreds or thousands of lives? I don't know how to respond to these curious people in a way that they would understand. There's no use trying to explain. Probably no one else would comprehend the reason for my decision as much as I do.

Never mind other people, you yourself, Mother, would probably fail to fathom the thought process that led to my actions. Even though the bond between the two of us—mother and son—was close and uncontentious, on occasion, you hurt my feelings. Your evil tongue was not as nice to me as it should have been. Sometimes when you smiled, your tongue nonetheless didn't smile with you. Sometimes when you asked after my wellbeing, your tongue nonetheless ridiculed my failure at work, kicked me when I was already down. Sometimes... when I wanted advice or moral support, your tongue nonetheless rebuffed me in a ruthless manner.

The time Nid drowned, your mouth rattled off

to everyone that it was an accident. But when you turned to me, your tongue was brandishing nonsense, dropping and spilling consonants and vowels as it lashed, so what ended up in my ears was no longer the word "accident;" it was another word, a word that has now been granted for my use without reservation. I don't deny it, Mother, that today I really am a murderer. Only I'm not fond of this word, I feel that it doesn't sound nice, it's not delicate on the senses, not pleasing to the ears, that's all.

But Nid's death is another matter. Oh Mother, how young was I then? Although I fought with her often— my sister with her pretty braids—no seeds of revenge were ever planted or ever grew within me; there was never any lingering grudge that would make me want to eliminate my dear little sister from this world. Let me tell you the honest truth, Mother. I loved Nid to death. Do you remember the time you spanked me so hard my backside turned burning red and then black and blue because I cracked the vanity mirror in your bedroom? Nid pointed her finger at me, and I bowed my head, taking the fall without protest, even though in truth I hadn't touched so much as a speck of dust on that mirror. I loved her, Mother, so I played the noble, protective older brother, shielding my sister from the consequences of her misbehaviors as much as situations and opportunities allowed. I was hurting, Mother. I was really hurting. My buttocks aren't made of steel. They're ordinary human flesh, the same flesh that you used to sprinkle with baby powder at bedtime. But to maintain my cute-as-a-button little sister's innocence in your eyes, I submitted myself as the wrongdoer in her place. I don't know how she felt about her big brother's heroic act. Not one word of thanks ever spilled from her lips, only laughter of satisfaction that someone else had to bear the punishment for the sin she herself committed. Still, I didn't mind, Mother. My love for her was unconditional. Even if Nid had loathed me to the bones, I would have persisted as her defender, protecting her from all manners of ill luck bent on intruding into her life. With love that strong, how could I have had the heart to stand by and watch her become overwhelmed by water, her respiratory path closing off and her heartbeat drowning out?

Impossible…

Do you recall how that day at the pool, before you disappeared into the house, you called out, "Keep a close eye on Nid, alright? She's not a strong swimmer yet. Watch her arm floaties—be careful they don't fall off." And then you went inside to call the doctor.

Given my charge, I was on alert, watching Nid as

if I were her personal security guard. I forwent playing in the water for my own amusement. I only stayed
put, standing by in the clear blue water, noting her
every move as she paddled herself back and forth in
circles along the surface. The fine spray that period-
ically splashed me in the face didn't bother this loyal
brother one bit. The sight of Nid's little body was
endearing. It won't be long, Nid, it won't be long
before you won't need to rely on those little floaties
on your arms anymore, I thought, smiling to myself.
Soon you're going to know how to swim. Using your
arms and legs to beat and kick the water, you'll be
able to propel yourself forward. The harder you go at
it, the faster you'll move. Plus, you'll be able to switch
and change to different strokes. You can even flip over
and lie back facing the sky. They call that the backstroke. But you don't have to swim the backstroke.
You can simply kick your feet one after the other
and keep your arms by the sides of your body, and
you'll be able to float along on your back for a good
while. It's such a nice and easy way to swim. I really
enjoy this one. I like feeling as though the water's simply carrying my body along. I just lie back, looking
at this and that, whatever there is to look at above.
Sometimes there are clouds, sometimes there aren't.
Sometimes there are only birds flying by, sometimes

there aren't.

Those were the thoughts that ran through my head as I carried out with dedication my duty of keeping an eye on Nid as you had instructed.

"Why aren't you swimming?" Nid stopped kicking the water as she asked me with that teensy little voice of hers that I can still hear to this day. You yourself know, Mother, that Nid was an inquisitive child, constantly curious. That was her special trait that I admired and partly envied. You can probably remember what a shy kid I was.

"Because Mama asked me to watch you." I never lie to anyone in the family.

"Where's Mama?"

I turned and gazed at the house, then turned back and replied, "She went in to give the doctor a call."

I admit I'd gathered that answer for myself. It wasn't as if I could see through cement walls. You could have been in the bathroom, or you could have been cooking. But during that period, I noticed that you talked to the doctor on the phone often. At the time, I didn't even know his name, which field of medicine he practiced, or why he had to come visit us at home almost every night. Some nights he didn't even leave until the next morning. I remember how the doctor volunteered to drive Nid and me to school in the morning on quite a few occasions. I didn't understand what his relationship was to our family. Why didn't we call him "uncle" or some such title the way we did with most other people? You told us to address him as "doctor," so I didn't mind addressing him that way, even though he never once treated me for anything.

"Is the doctor coming over to see us again?" Nid asked as she flapped her arms in the water around her, left once, right once, taking her body along the side of the pool, floating toward the spot where I was standing.

"I don't know." Because I didn't know, Mother.

"Is the doctor our dad?" Nid pinched her nose with her tiny right hand—probably pressure from the chlorine had worked its way into her nasal passage.

"No. Why?"

"Sometimes the doctor takes us out. My friends' dads take them out."

I never thought that the doctor driving us places amounted to his taking us out. Going out has to be fun. He never took us out for fun.

"Just keep playing there, Nid. Mama will be out soon." I didn't like talking about the doctor.

"It's not fun to play by myself. Will you give me a lift on your shoulders?"

"No." Having a human body wrapped around my neck wasn't something I enjoyed, not even if that body belonged to Nid.

"Then what game should we play? I want to play a game." Nid started to pull a sour expression, and her face immediately lost its cuteness.

After a moment's reflection, I proposed: "Let's have a hold-your-breath contest. Whoever keeps their face under water the longest wins."

Ever since that day's unimaginable incident, I began to notice your tongue's hostility toward me. You could be praising me for anything, and no matter what it was, your darn tongue would twist and turn your beautiful words into something grating to my ears every time.

It's because of you and your tongue that everyone in the Kingdom of Siam knows who I am. You can be sure that there's not a single person who hasn't heard our story over the past week. This awkward face you've known straight out of the womb has been plastered over and over again on the pages of every newspaper. My name is more often on people's tongues than those of the current chart-topping pop stars. Turn on any TV, be it black-and-white or color, and spend a short while in front of the screen, and I guarantee this familiar face will make an appearance.

Switch on any radio, if you don't hear music, you'll hear an update on your son's scandalous trial.

I'm going to be executed by gunshot! If this news could reach you, how would it make you feel?

As for me, I'm not particularly perturbed. It's fitting: with a murder so gruesome, there is only one punishment that fits the crime.

I wish you could read the headlines about my case—these journalists are so creative and so eloquent. When you read them, you can really visualize along with the words. There's one I particularly like. It's simple, concise, and contains almost all the key pieces of information. Readers don't have to bother glancing down further for details:

"Deranged, Heartless Son Butchers Mother, Stuffs Bits in Garbage."

I forgot to ask you, Mother—did it hurt? It probably didn't hurt one bit, right? I released my grip on your neck only when I was sure that any sign of struggling had left your body, that there was no way you could feel any more pain.

Butchering a human body is no simple task, and to be frank, I never intended to have to wrestle so hard. All I really wanted was your evil tongue. It was the only organ I wanted to eliminate from my sight. But once I had your tongue sliced out, I was emboldened and wanted to play doctor like some other people. Besides, the bathroom floor was already stained and needed to be washed and scrubbed anyway.

Even now, all those curious people, not one of them knows where your tongue has disappeared to.

The reason they don't know is… I won't tell.

I'm leaving it as a mystery for the media to have something to keep investigating.

I'm hungry now, Mother. It's getting closer and closer to noon. I'll probably take the opportunity to give my hand a rest here. If I feel inspired and I'm not disturbed by so many people making demands on my time as in previous days, I'll get back to writing some more this afternoon.

Oh, one little postscript.

I just remembered the last sentence I uttered to Nid in the pool.

She asked me, "Why can't people open their mouths and talk under water?"

I answered: "Because water doesn't like people who talk too much."

Even though I fibbed a little, it didn't matter.

Did it?

PART 3: DESTINY'S A DICK

The slamming of the door to room seventeen jolted Meuy awake.

The cream-colored synthetic-leather seat underneath her nineteen-year-old's behind gave off a stench of waiting, culled together from people of various sorts, with Meuy being the latest person to contribute a specimen to this cheap piece of furniture.

The knockoff Rolex on her left wrist—price tag, two hundred and fifty baht—had its dial turned to be within its owner's eyeshot. It was reportedly 1:13 in the morning.

Which she believed.

Some places in the world don't exist on official maps. This pink-walled motel was one of them. The world outside could zoom in any direction, but when night fell, a multitude of men seeking to satisfy their instinct came by to visit the world of lust. If prostitution is the world's oldest profession, as they say, then the pink motel was akin to an important museum, preserving the trade that has escorted civilization through time, ensuring the perpetuation of pleasure as it continues its course.

The setup was simple, but it managed to meet its users' needs without having to struggle to evolve with the times. Each customer wanted only a bit of convenience so that the deed could be done within an hour or so. The pink motel, therefore, didn't need a swimming pool, a meeting room or any of the usual amenities for business dealings. Each room contained only a bed and a bathroom, the two main necessities for the business of selling love. Even televisions, often provided as a free amenity, could be considered a wasteful extravagance in this case.

But it was this extravagance that Meuy appreciated the most in the course of the performance of her work.

The television functioned as an object that connected the world within the pink walls to the world outside. For Meuy, it lifted some of the tension and dread off her mind: at least she could take comfort in the fact that millions of people outside these walls were engrossed by the display on screen, sucked in by the same soap opera as she was. Even if the man fondling her and feeling her up—grabbing and groping

her naked body—was a stranger, the moving image of
a familiar star on the oblong screen made her feel safe.

Her series of the moment had already aired earlier in the evening, when she was still sashaying and
swinging around a metal pole at a bar in the vicinity.
Sunday evening was rather slow; she hadn't escorted
a single customer back to a room, so she missed the
verbal showdown between the leading lady and the
jealous villainess that she'd been waiting to see for
weeks. "It was fucking fierce, Meuy," a friend in the
same line of work yelled to her from across the road
over the traffic when she was just a few steps out of
the bar. "There was almost some slap action but the
damn show went and ended first. Next week there's
definitely going to be some lip-splitting."

"For real?" Meuy shouted back with genuine
interest.

"Oh! More real than a tranny's boobs. There were
serious waterworks, too. And the mother-in-law was
on hand to help lay it on heavy. You missed a major
moment, bitch, believe me."

Which Meuy believed.

Meuy continued down the sidewalk, her head
hanging with disappointment. And what she'd made
tonight was chump change, nothing worth standing
there for hours baring her flesh and shaking her limbs

in front of the nocturnal public for. To add insult to injury, she had to miss a big episode of her favorite soap (the leading lady of which, by her own private estimation, bore a dead-on resemblance to her— it was exactly as if she were looking in the mirror, except the Meuy in her reflection led a life so much more splendid than the real Meuy that the comparison between them was like the open sky and the pit of the earth.)

The time then was only a few minutes past midnight. The night was still young for those who lived off the hours after dark. Meuy didn't want to head back to her room yet, but she'd had it with the pole at the bar and couldn't bear to twirl herself around the damn thing any longer. Tonight, she wanted to let herself come down and stand on the same level as the other citizens of the world. Then tomorrow she'd return to the stage to expose her flesh once again, because whatever happened, the show must go on, as they say in English.

Downcast and demoralized, she spilled these emotions along the sidewalk as she strolled. But just then her cell phone started to ring inside the three-hundred-and-twenty-baht black Prada bag hanging from the crook of her left arm.

Meuy reached in for the communication device

and pressed the key allowing the other side to radio through to her. Hearing a familiar voice, she greeted the caller casually: "Yeah, I left. Got lazy. And have had it to here. And I missed the show. Bummer. And it was chilly. I don't know. I don't want to go back but I don't know what to do with myself. And I haven't made any money. Oh, yeah? Oh, sounds good. I'll come over then. You're sure there are clients?"

That was the conversation between Meuy and Aim.

Aim worked as a cashier at the pink-walled motel, a melting pot of different cultures that was more hopping than a United Nations meeting. Each night, people came by to use its services, convening from an assortment of continents and places. The glass door in front of the reception area was soiled with the handprints of people of various nationalities and races; they pushed it forward, passed through, and entered with the same purpose, despite their disparate backgrounds. Here... the pink motel! Few people paid attention to what it was actually called. As a matter of fact, it had a fancy English name, written in bright white oil paint above the entrance: PARADISE LOTS, an admirable turn at a riff on *Paradise Lost*, that classic of western literature. The person who came up with it was likely a foreigner gifted with wit and intellect.

Here was proof that free knowledge could be found anywhere, even above the door to a whorehouse—a genuine oasis of peace, a place full of truths. Whoever saw it as a den of illegality clearly hadn't been enlightened to the fact that all eternal truths in human life were illicit.

The conversation reported earlier between Meuy and Aim contained only Meuy's side of the exchange. For the sake of social justice, the words that Aim served up should be revealed here too, as follows:

"Hey, Meuy, are you already out? You're not dancing anymore? Ah. Yeah? A-ha. What are you up to then? You're gonna go home? Yeah, why don't you come hang out in the motel lobby then? There are a lot of guests today. Maybe you'll catch one. Just now some came and sat around, and a bunch of them got some. Yeah, come. You can hang here and keep me company if nothing else."

Which is how Meuy ended up on the cream-colored synthetic-leather sofa, where she'd been nodding off since around 12:30 a.m. For her part, the young female cashier named Aim sat there counting up cash and periodically making conversation with her friend from behind the plywood counter painted in bright turquoise, which popped mightily against the pink of the walls. Above Aim's head was an old, out-of-style poster of a raging white horse rearing up in front of a high waterfall. To Aim's left, aside from the plastic baskets for change and candy wrappers, there were boxes of the number-one brand for condoms stacked in a column about as high as a soda can. The reason the height of the prophylactics column could be so concretely described was thanks to the can of grape soda to Aim's right, just waiting to be put to such use. Aim took one glance at the stack of condoms, and, shifting her eyes to the right, one glance at the soda can. Then she made the following observation in her head: six condom boxes equal one soda can. That was autodidact education, Aim style.

From the time Meuy eased her behind onto the sofa, a client had yet to enter in search of a pleasure fuse. There were some who came through, but these guests had packed their own fuses from elsewhere, and they headed straight into the various rooms, arms linked or hands locked with their companions, ready to have their firecrackers expertly set off. The men didn't even so much as look Meuy's way, her body languidly awaiting, seeking attention in the lobby.

A mixture of fatigue and ennui caused a chemical reaction within the young woman, making her eye-lids feel heavier than usual. Even though her body was still open for business, above the neck, certain facial sense organs fought hard to shut down.

Until the door to room seventeen slammed—bang!

As soon as her eyes flicked open, jolted by the crashing sound, she detected a snickering from behind the counter.

"What the hell are you laughing at? I'm sleepy," Meuy grumbled as she straightened up and adjusted her tight black skirt by pulling at the hem.

"I'm not laughing at you," Aim said, sounding amused. She hadn't even noticed that her friend had dozed off for several minutes. "I'm laughing at Hia Nuad."

"Who?" Meuy asked, although she wasn't seriously interested. With her right hand, she fished a lipstick out of her Prada bag, and then reached in again to feel for her compact.

"Mr. Nuad, the guy with the mustache who went into room seventeen just now." Aim barely got her explanation out before her right hand covered her mouth in an attempt to muffle the sound of laughter spilling out of it.

"Is he so funny or something? What country is he from?"

"He's Thai." After she almost suffocated a couple of times from laughing so hard, Aim inhaled deeply into her lungs. "He started visiting a lot in the last two or three days. He pays for the room, then he goes in and sits alone for a bit over an hour, and then he goes home."

"That's more weird than it is funny, I think," Meuy said, her voice barely audible. Her eyes were preoccupied with the reflection of her orange-red pout in the tiny compact mirror, as she ran lipstick along its full curves, freshening the color.

"Oh, you don't know yet why I'm laughing," Aim widened her eyes, and a devious smile appeared below the apples of her cheeks.

"And when are you going to tell me? I'm dolling myself up in anticipation here." Meuy closed her compact and dropped it, together with her rouge, back into the dark cavern of her bag. Having finished, she looked up at her girlfriend behind the counter, ready to face whatever strange tale the latter had to impart.

Aim waved Meuy over to her.

"I gotta get up?" Meuy's eyebrows closed in on each other in displeasure before her backside lifted from the seat and swung its way through space toward the destination ahead. The black bag was left behind.

At the counter, Meuy rested both her arms on the edge and craned her neck toward the cashier girl. "Is the moment auspicious enough yet?"

Aim put her head so close to her friend's that their breaths were starting to encroach on each other's territory. From there, she began in a conspiratorial whisper.

"That Hia Nuad, they say he doesn't have that thing."

Meuy didn't understand. "What thing? What doesn't he have?"

Aim tilted her face downward about forty-five degrees and aimed her right index finger at her crotch. "That thing, you moron."

Meuy followed Aim's cue with her eyes. Once she got the picture—of that certain organ—it made her exclaim wordlessly and cover her mouth, certain that her heart would fall to the floor.

"You're crazy! Who told you? How could he not have one? Can you lose it, that thing?"

"For real! He took a girl in with him once. Her name's Oy or something. She was in there for probably half an hour, and she came out looking completely disgusted. She said to me, Hia Nuad doesn't have a you-know-what." Even though Aim was moving her lips gingerly and in a hush, the background silence of the room wasn't conducive to keeping secrets, so her whispers appeared to be several decibels louder than usual.

Meuy was incredulous. "How is that possible? What hole is he supposed to piss through?" Her eyes were filled with confusion.

"Let me finish the story," Aim gave Meuy a wave-off, providing her own frustration an outlet. "The girl told me, where that thing's supposed to be, Hia Nuad has a little tube sticking out instead."

Meuy's face bunched up immediately: Aim's words had morphed into an unpalatable image floating in her head.

"And…" Meuy dragged the word out real long, before picking up with, "How does he do it? Does he use the tube?"

"Oy said he just stood there and watched her shower. He didn't do anything. When she was done, he asked her to roll around on the bed for a while, and then he kicked her out, told her she could go."

"Did he pay her?"

"Of course. In full, too."

"And…" It was the second "and" that Meuy dragged out while the gears in her head turned. "How did he lose it?"

"How the hell am I supposed to know? Probably someone chopped it off."

The nineteen-year-old girl tugged her skirt down taut, her brain still engrossed in the hideous image that was starting to take a clear and concrete form somewhere inside her mind.

Aim stared hard at Meuy's face, as if she were analyzing a fellow human's thought process.

Eventually, Meuy expressed her resolution out loud, "I don't buy it. You got hoaxed by that little hoe. Or you're pulling my leg."

"It's almost two in the morning—that's past the hour for pranking a friend. Why the fuck would I want to trick you? It's not just that Oy. Aunt Jerd's seen it, too." Jerd was one of four cleaners at the pink-walled motel. "Aunt Jerd went into Hia Nuad's room accidentally, and he happened to be standing in there, butt naked. She bolted immediately. She confirmed Oy's story, every element of it."

"Where is Aunt Jerd? I want to ask her myself." Meuy looked around. In a space that tiny, even if Jerd were a dwarf, you'd have noticed if she was there. But there was only the two of them in the lobby, and the clatter that snuck out through the door cracks occasionally from the twenty rooms that lined up to the west of where Meuy was sitting.

"Today's her day off," Aim said, speaking in a normal voice now, having whispered with her lips scrunched for several minutes. Then she sat her butt back down on the chair at her station.

"Uh-huh, how convenient. And how am I supposed to find out if what you told me is true?"

"There's a way," Aim sounded mildly irritated. "You can go ask him."

For a moment, Meuy was taken aback by her friend's suggestion. She turned her head in the direction of room seventeen and then zoomed in, following the hallway with her eyes, scouting the path lined with shoddy carpeting in muddled maroon. Only a few paces away, the answer and the truth were awaiting a knock.

She mobilized her legs and held her head straight, determined to make the trip to test the truth of Aim's story.

Among the light-blue doors separated by pink walls, Meuy passed number one (left) and number eleven (right), numbers two and twelve, three and thirteen, and so on, until she was coming up on numbers seven and seventeen.

"She's doing it for real, that crazy bitch," Aim mumbled to herself as she followed her friend's footsteps with her gaze.

And finally Meuy stopped between two doors. The one on the left was room seven; the one on the right was Hia Nuad's room. Turing to face her target, she gulped first and then her right hand reached toward the rectangular panel of wood.

She landed her fist on the door three times; three clear, loud knocks.

Hia Nuad, a Thai man of Chinese descent, was in his early forties or so. Mid-trunk, he had a belly protruding to the front. While the hair on his head was buzzed short, he had dense, dark hair under his nose, which obscured the outline of his upper lip. The mustache was likely the origin of his moniker, Nuad. Presently, his top half was unclothed, while his bottom half was wrapped in a thin white towel.

Inside the room, a blue light from the TV screen flickered, casting a wall-to-wall glow. The noise in the background was a familiar one—it fit the formula for videos demonstrating how people of the world engage in sex. The group performing the on-screen demonstration in Hia Nuad's room was probably Japanese, Meuy reckoned from the characteristic sounds that rippled into her ears. Other than that, there was no trace of another human being in room seventeen.

"Can I help you?" Hia Nuad eyed Meuy suspiciously.

"Excuse me," Meuy put her hands in prayer in front of her chest. "I have something I want to clear up, something that I want to ask you about."

"What is it? Who are you?" Hia Nuad poked his

head out beyond the threshold and turned to glance at the lobby area.

"My name's Jiab"—her professional handle—"My friend said…" The girl with two names kept her palms pressed firmly together. "My friend said…" Some questions are hard to spit out.

"What? Get on with it. I've already paid for the room so don't waste my time."

"So… my friend…" So, her friend something. Meuy couldn't yet string the words together in her head.

"The hemming and hawing—what is this?" Hia Nuad grabbed the doorknob, ready to push the door back into its frame.

"So… my friend said," Meuy paused and gulped before continuing, "She said you don't have that thing—is it true?" Her head bowed slightly, palms already joined, she appeared to be giving an elder a wai as if to ask for forgiveness.

The first thing to register on Hia Nuad's face was utter shock. All the blood that nourished his cheeks and gave them some plumpness decided at once to drain down to the bottom of the earth. What followed next was his body becoming possessed in its entirety by a soul of pain. His legs trembled; the joints that once secured his stance as a two-legged animal felt like they were slowly drooping and about to give. His eyebrows which once stood so erect that they rippled the skin on his forehead now sagged almost to his lash lines. Soon the dam confining the fluid of despair collapsed spectacularly, and the man of over forty years of age had to use both palms to block the gush of liquid streaming out of his eyes.

Before door number seventeen banged shut, Meuy noticed Hia Nuad's eyes, looking at her sidelong, appearing to be begging for compassion.

The teenaged girl stood frozen to her spot.

She was exhausted, she was fed up, she was sleepy. She'd made no money, and on top of that, she'd made a grown-up cry.

That was what destiny had in store for Miss Meuy that night.

PART 4: FEET FIRST

Swish!

The Bluebird whooshes by the tip of the three-horned demon's nose, leaving a black trail in the air.

Frup! The demon grabs at the Bluebird with its enormous hands.

Oooph! The Bluebird narrowly escapes its pounce.

Floosh! The Bluebird does a three-sixty flip before zooming through the clouds.

Beep, beep. A radio signal goes off in the spaceship. "Bluebird, Bluebird. Black Dog to Bluebird. Death Chanter's wreaking havoc in the middle of the city. Over." Looking stern is Captain Blue, Knight of the Universe Number Nine, Captain of the noble Bluebird Spaceship. The thought in his head: dot, dot, dot. His right temple is dripping huge beads of sweat that don't quite drop from his face, or off the page.

"Bluebird here. Copy and over!" Captain Blue says into the communication device held up to his mouth.

Shmm! The metal spaceship does a flip mid-air, heading right for the demon's body. "I'm sorry, demon, but I have a lot of other business to take care of. I can't be dillydallying with you. Now die!"

Bzzzt! Fooooom! The Bluebird shoots out a squiggly beam of light. Shackled by the Blue Ray, the three-horned demon gapes its mouth open in agony and collapses onto the ground when the beam fades out. Crash! Boom!

"Argh!" It lets out a last groan through its jagged fangs. Swish! The Bluebird zips through the sky, heading for the next mission that awaits in the heart of the city...

"Ha-ham!" Roang cleared his throat. And as he blocked the expelled air with his right hand, as a reflex he took his eyes off the Captain Blue comic book in his other hand.

The sky having been gloomy since the afternoon, the natural dimness that accompanied the hour a little past 6 p.m. was rendered rather superfluous. To avoid having to face the rain or expose his body to it, Roang had decided to go home instead of monkeying around with his friends after school as he usually did. He'd rather not have sloshed around in sopping wet shoes all the way home if he could help it.

As he walked, his backpack bobbed up and down a little from the impact. The light-brown sneakers on his feet moved with pep at a steady pace down the narrow alley. The sand-paved passageway was a bit like a ditch, wedged between the walls of two office buildings' parking garages that left a gap between them. Roang liked to use this unclaimed channel as a shortcut to the dock for the ferry, the means of transportation that shuttled the eighth-grader between his home life and his school life, back and forth every day.

Ha-ham! His throat was still scratchy. Please don't let me get a cold, Roang prayed. In a few weeks, his life was about to be cloaked by the dark cloud of final exams. Since the start of the semester, he hadn't once cracked his schoolbooks open to review the material. The future was closing in on him, and he'd been intending to dedicate what little time he had left to applying himself. He needed to squeeze and scrape out the knowledge that he had collected in the crevices of his brain and force it to resurface to memory. If he were to get sick now, where was he supposed to find the strength and the stamina to fight the tough war…?

"Black Dog to Bluebird. The situation's getting worse by the second. A great number of people have fallen under the demon's spell. It won't be long before its deadly power makes people kill each other. Come to the rescue, quick!" Captain Black's face is studded with ten or so beads of sweat. Around him, the atmosphere is somber, jam-packed with dark vertical lines and nothing else. Froom! The Bluebird is still gliding through the skyscape, grand and dignified, its speed cutting a line midair.

"On my way! Over!" Captain Blue yells into the microphone, his Adam's apple wiggling. Uzzzz! Zap! Death Chanter unleashes its mind-control waves on the ordinary people on the street, aiming for the crowns of their heads. Those under its spell exhibit black circles around their eyes, stiffened hands, and zombie-like movements. Ugh! Pow! Some are starting to attack each other.

Swish! Under Captain Blue's navigation, the Bluebird is now soaring above the scene...

Woof! An angry dog made its presence known from behind, setting off Roang's curiosity. He took his eyes off the action on the page again and turned around to investigate the source of the barking.

The barker had disappeared somewhere (or was he hearing things?). What he saw was a man with a tiny frame, his hair buzzed on the sides, in his twenties, maybe. He wore a black short-sleeved button-down shirt over a pair of beat-up jeans. In his right hand, the man had a clear glass bottle that appeared not to hold any liquid. He took creeping steps, as if he were counting each one. His head hung low, his gaze likely fixed to the ground.

Roang and the man with the bottle were the only ones on the path. Roang was halfway down the alley, whereas the man had just approached, not more than a few steps in.

Roang's heels, warm inside the sneakers that met every requirement of school regulations, started to twitch. He had never felt his heels jerk like that before. He had never imagined they could do that, and if they really could, he was at his wit's end as to why they were doing so now.

Krr! The Bluebird is gradually descending.

"Bluebird to Black Dog. I've arrived. Decreasing altitude to locate the demon," Captain Blue's voice emanates from the spaceship.

"Bluebird! You made good time. Death Chanter is standing by the intersection near the gas station. It has shrunk itself down to human size to conserve its power. Likely, the mind-control waves drained its body significantly. Black Dog's systems were severely damaged in the face-off. I can't move it. I'm afraid I'm going to have to leave the responsibility entirely to you, Bluebird. The world's survival depends on you! I'm leaving it in your hands."

Krr! The Bluebird is still slowly lowering down. Whoosh! Death Chanter turns and spots the arrival, which makes three giant exclamation points in a row pop up above its head (!!!). "I've ascertained Death Chanter's coordinates," Captain Blue announces.

Roang's heels twitched again. This time they were pulsing like beats normally felt in the chest. Bewildered, he stopped walking, but the twitching refused to let up.

Roang lifted his left foot, flipping it sideways for inspection. He tried to imagine as he studied it that his eyes had X-ray powers and could penetrate through his skin to identify the problem. But he could have carried on staring at his foot until the world drowned in an apocalyptic flood, and he still wouldn't have stood a chance of seeing even so much as his own skin, what with the sneaker and sock still obstructing his view. Roang was no dummy, so he returned his foot to its appropriate position and continued walking, leaving two mysteries hanging over his head.

First: Why were his heels twitching?

Second: How close was the man with the glass bottle now? (The answer to this question was not hard to find out. If Roang only turned to look, he would certainly no longer have to wonder. But with his mind still wrapped in the comic book, he wasn't able to mobilize the muscles above his shoulders, which he very much needed to do in order to turn—Captain Blue was waiting for him after all.)

Krrr! Krrr! The Bluebird is landing on a wide street near an intersection. Thump! At last, it makes contact with the concrete. Squeak! The spaceship door opens, revealing the commanding figure of Captain Blue, standing tall with a black cape flapping behind him. Uzzz! Death Chanter is taken back, having long heard other demons' fearsome stories about the knight's countless heroic deeds. Captain Blue has round eyes that sparkle and wispy hair that flops down, its pointy ends curving with the wind. He jumps down from the spaceship— swoosh!—and within a single panel Captain Blue has already charged his way within striking distance of the demon.

"Death Chanter, it's time for your atrocities to end. Release the minds of these innocent people from your evil spell now." Gulp, the demon swallows its saliva. But how could it surrender without a fight? It is after all a demon, not some lowly snatch-and-run pickpocket hanging around a bus stop.

"Hahaha. Captain Blue, finally we meet. I feel quite honored to be verbally sparring face-to-face like this with the renowned Knight of the Universe. Too bad for you, I fear we can't exchange any more rhetoric because I'm not in the mood to chat. I'd rather get on with taking over the world—I must eliminate you now so nothing stands in my way." Zap! A huge beam of light shoots out from the demon's palm at Captain Blue's body.

Plop! The captain jumps out of harm's way in time, leaving a cloud of dust in his place. "Do you think a lame move like that can intimidate Captain Blue, Protector of the Universe?" He sneers, his eyes still every bit as sparkling as before. Hrumph, the demon clenches its teeth, its face becoming even more hideous, three beads of sweat taking form on its temples from sheer anxiety.

"Ha! The bravado! Wait until you get a taste of my mind control." Such confidence in the demon's voice has even Captain Blue flabbergasted, his thought bubble full of dot, dot, dot.

Smassh! Roang's earlobes nearly vibrated when the sound of trouble struck him. He was sure the origin for it was the shattering of the glass bottle the man behind him held in his hand, but he didn't want to rush to conclusions as to why it had broken. He decided to keep this vexing issue tucked away in his mind for now, even though the muscles in his heels were pulsating with a greater sense of panic by the second, as though they were expanding and on their way to exploding.

Captain Blue is in danger.

Blap! Looking left and right, the captain almost can't believe his eyes: an onslaught of ordinary people, over a hundred of them, are moving in on him, and they certainly do not look like they're coming in peace. Stomp! Stomp! With their pairs upon pairs of legs, they are marching almost like an army, all headed for the same target: Captain Blue.

"Hahaha!" Death Chanter laughs, baring its fangs. "Let's see what you do now. These are the innocent people you want to defend and protect, but they are such ingrates. They even have the heart to kill Captain Blue, Protector of the Universe. Hahaha!"

Captain Blue deliberated hard while he stood there as a non-moving target. With his right hand on his tapered chin, he let out a hmmm.

Tmp, tmp, tmp. Roang caught himself swinging his legs at a faster pace than what could be called walking, despite the fact that no part of his brain had signaled his legs to plow through the air so hard. But he was running—there was no mistaking it because he was looking down, astonished, at his two feet as they took turns flinging rapidly forward on the sand.

He had no idea why his feet had started running, he didn't know what had ordered them to do so, but running he certainly was. Tmp, tmp, tmp. The visuals and the sound were both there, so he wasn't imagining it.

Tmp, tmp, tmp. The sound of foreign footsteps now added to his own.

Blap! Glancing back, Roang saw the most terrifying sight he had ever laid eyes on—even Death Chanter's beastly face couldn't compete.

The man who, just a few minutes ago, had been passively walking behind him in the alley had now morphed into a ferocious predator charging at him, chasing after him with the speed of a jet stream. In his hand, he was brandishing the glass bottle that had been cracked into a sharp and dangerous weapon; his eyes were widened but contained no trace of a soul; and he was foaming at the mouth, his drool dribbling down in long, transparent strands that split and splattered when hit by the wind.

Although Roang was still puzzled as to how his feet could order his legs to start sprinting all by themselves, when he saw what was hot on his heels, he immediately felt thankful for the feet's decision. If he had still been taking a leisurely stroll reading his comic book, who knows how many cuts he would have endured by now? He might even already be lying in a pool of blood, groaning in pain.

Roang tightened his grip on the tale of Captain Blue's struggle against injustice and concentrated harder on running. A few more steps and he would reach the path along the canal that would lead him to the dock.

Rumble! Rumble! Rumble! The sky roared, threatening from every direction.

The faster Roang sprinted, the more it seemed the madman behind him was catching up, showing superior power. As Roang's heart pounded, his temples thumped with pain that was spreading through the whole of his head.

Dub, dub. Lub, lub. Bpum, bpum. Roang sprang forward, sending his body onto the concrete walkway along the canal. Finally, he had made it out of that narrow alley.

When he heard the ferry cruising in, gliding along the water, he was able to breathe several more sighs of relief. Clap! Crack! Rumble, rumble, rumble. Crackle, crackle. Tilting his head up, he saw a cluster of dark clouds, but didn't feel any raindrops yet. When he looked back down, what he saw out of the corner of his eye to the left was the ferry, packed with passengers, about to dock ahead—that image was enough to bring a little smile to his face. Wanting to leap straight onto the boat without decelerating, he tried to coax the force of motion in his body to reveal itself once again.

Thump! He succeeded. Both his feet were planted on the wooden floor by the bow, the impact of his jump rocking the boat a bit.

"Take it away, sir! That guy's trying to hurt me," Roang yelled in the direction of the skipper as he rolled his comic book and pointed it at the madman who was standing several steps away from the dock, brows furrowed over his angry, vindictive face. The skipper appeared unfazed by Roang's dramatic entrance, but he was willing to rev up the engine and pull away without having come to a complete stop. It was his good fortune that none of the passengers wanted to get off at that station, Roang thought quietly.

"Psycho," he muttered flatly to himself. Although he didn't understand what had transpired, as long as he felt safe now, that was enough. He was standing in the same spot on the boat as where he had first landed, his hand holding on to the nylon guard rope. He hadn't looked back to check on the status of the man on the riverbank, and it hadn't at all crossed his mind as strange that not one of the other passengers had paid him any attention. Even the boat conductor didn't seem interested in coming over to collect his fare. Everyone was sitting still, their eyes gazing blankly ahead.

Rumble, rumble, rumble. The roars from above were coming in at increasingly shorter intervals now. In his heels, Roang still felt a twitching.

Annoyed, he turned his attention away from the strange symptom in his shoes and back to Captain Blue's adventures on the page.

Wham! Captain Blue manages to break away from the mob of one-hundred-plus zombies. Flub! The Knight of the Universe's cape is billowing once again.

"To save these innocent lives, I have to end yours right now." Captain Blue points his finger at Death Chanter.

"Do you think it's going to be so easy to kill me, Captain Blue?" The demon smiles sweetly but cunningly. "Since I can control this worthless bunch, why wouldn't my mind control work on you!" Zap! Zap! From its body, Death Chanter unleashes its glowing beam of mind control on Captain Blue. "No!" "Argh!" "Don't!" The knight is ensnared by the force of the demon. What becomes of the world, find out in the next volume.

"Oh, it's already the end!" Roang grumbled to

himself. He closed the book and looked down at his feet once again.

What the…? Why are they still twitching? There's nowhere to run this time—there's only getting soaked.

Clatter. Clat. Clat. The heels were quivering more and more forcefully.

Because he was preoccupied with his lower extremities, Roang hadn't thought to take note of the conduct of the other passengers on the boat.

All eyes were on him now, every pair of their dark, cold, soulless eyes. An instant later, a low, coordinated chant issued from every one of their windpipes:

"Kill. Kill. Kill. Kill. Kill."

Rumble. Rumble. Rumble.

Splash!

As if it had been struck by a bomb, one spot in the brown canal blew up.

Roang's two feet kicked and crawled in the water.

Slosh, slosh, slosh.

PART 5: MOCK TAIL

Shamada had already tossed her soiled white socks into the laundry hamper, but in the end she changed her mind about jumping in the shower. In that moment, the brainwaves firing in her head were making her giddy, giggly even, and her quickened breath was giving her a rush, all these elements charging at her so hard that the eighteen-year-old was teetering on nausea. So these were the symptoms of anticipation leading up to the great excitement of a hot-blooded young woman's life?

She belly-flopped onto her soft bed, her weight kicking up the slight layer of dust that had settled during the day. The soles of her bare feet were facing toward the ceiling, and her chin, gently rounded, was cupped in her right palm, her gaze turned toward the nightstand. Along with the pale-yellow ceramic lamp, the pink alarm clock, the plastic piggy bank in the form of a panda's head, two rubber bands and three plain silver barrettes, the top of the mini-table was also adorned with another item whose importance rose above everything else's: the square wooden frame standing next to the base of the lamp. It had been painstakingly positioned so that it would catch the amber beam from her night lamp at an angle Shamada had deemed loveliest.

If a picture frame were without a picture, its status as such would be incomplete and, by implication, it would become a pointless object. But Shamada's frame naturally housed a photograph, and, moreover, it was a photograph she loved and treasured as much as a girl could treasure an inanimate object.

And the person in the photo? He was no stranger or common celebrity whose picture can be clipped from a magazine by anyone with a pair of scissors. The two-dimensional young heartthrob in the picture was standing with his arms crossed over his chest, exuding swoon-inducing charm through the dimples at the base of his cheeks. It was plain to see he could be the object of desire of hordes of girls. His name was Komtal, and what was more, he held the title of being Shamada's darling sweet angel.

Tomorrow was the third anniversary of the day Shamada had first let Komtal take her by the arm and hold her by the hand. A variety of other interactions besides being arm in arm and hand in hand had ensued since then—that was par for the course for lovers—but for a girl to give the play-by-play would be unseemly, and, anyway, Shamada blushed easily. If she had to spill the beans on the delicate matters that went on between her and her oh-so-fine beau with the level of detail where you could picture the scenes and imagine the sounds, she feared that her round cheeks, fair as cotton balls, would turn bright red and combust.

Still, she might be able to work up the courage to give those interested a little peek of something, something that in fact hadn't happened between her and Komtal—but was about to.

"Komtal," the girl said out loud, even though there was no one else in the room to listen. She was presumably conversing with the photo in the frame because her face and her glance clearly pointed in that direction. Sometimes people get the urge to open their mouths and talk out loud to themselves, after having to carry on a monologue in their heads for the better part of the day.

"Komtal… (At last, I have faith in our relationship like never before. During our past three years together, all of your fine qualities and your through-and-through gentlemanliness have proved to me—I'm convinced of this deep in my heart—that I haven't chosen the wrong guy. You're the one who's going to be able to hold me up, look after me and protect me forever and ever. Since I'm so certain—tomorrow, to show my appreciation for your wonderful being, I'm going to gladly give my whole self to you as a gift. All of my anxieties, the worries about not being ready, they've completely faded away now. I don't even feel afraid. At this moment, my heart is filled with nothing but happiness and excitement. I can hardly wait any longer to be yours. The seconds that used to zoom by are now creeping so frustratingly slowly. The minutes that used to be short are now so excruciatingly long. And then there are the hours. How many lifetimes are they going to waste with their idle crawling? It'll be torture tonight, lying here waiting for the morning to roll in so I can see your face, touch you and love you as my heart desires.)"

Shamada pronounced only the name of her beloved out loud. Everything in parentheses was a pining that she continued in her head.

For an average girl, the apprehension over losing her virginity couldn't stray far from a certain body part that would be invaded and explored for the first time. But Shamada had a different body part that had been causing her distress deep inside for a long time.

Very few people knew that she, a girl endowed with such a flawlessly beautiful face and figure, harbored an inferiority complex, a secret even.

Shamada had no tail!

She was one of those mock tails! A strap-on wearer!

The long, sleek object that dangled gracefully from her behind like an elephant's trunk was a prosthetic tail that her father had sprung six figures for. He had had it custom-made in Germany right after his daughter slipped out of the womb to prevent her becoming the butt of malicious gossip. Her father sought out prosthetic tails of various sizes that could be affixed so seamlessly that no one would suspect that the lovely young lady had a physical handicap. Indeed, Shamada herself had never experienced the cruelty of living without a tail. When she grew old enough to have heard and understood the meaning of the term "mock tail,"—even then—back when she was still in the dark and thought herself "normal" like the average person walking on the street, she herself used to look down on the mock tails as a group of people cursed by heaven to be born lowly, creatures with a disability. She used to loathe having to walk past the strap-on wearers who loitered in packs around narrow alleys. She once laughed at a mock-tailed man who had literally been kicked off a fast-moving bus by a bunch of hot-headed university students. "Hahaha," she sneered, calling her parents to look at the sorry shape the unfortunate mock-tailed guy lay in: on the ground clutching his knees, rolling in pain as traffic flowed by.

One night when she was still a young girl, her father confessed to Shamada that the tail hanging from above her buttocks was not a true tail, but merely the tail of a hybrid animal that had been pruned and primed to simulate a human tail—the handiwork of a foreign expert. The tail had been loosely sewn to her skin and had to be replaced as her body grew. "That is, you're a mock tail," her father was telling her.

From that day, Shamada had to swallow the bitter pill of truth that she found difficult to share with others. She was a mock tail. She was like those people she had once ridiculed. What happened to the mock-tailed man on the public bus, could happen to her at any time if people around her realized that her tail was essentially a strap-on.

The prejudice she used to hold against mock tails, the internalized popular opinion of society, then turned into sympathy, into the desire to lend a helping hand to that group of unfortunate people—akin to a measure of tending to her own feelings and subconscious. Most mock tails didn't have sufficient financial means to maintain a faux tail like hers. Shamada therefore felt guilty the entire time she was able to conduct her life without a hitch, even though in truth she herself should have been facing the same fate as the other mock tails. She was fully cognizant of the inequity, and every day her heart ached in secret for the mock tails. But with regard to herself, Shamada was not quite ready to announce the truth to the world. She was not ready to drag herself down with them.

"Komtal—tomorrow, not only will I gladly become yours, I also have something extraordinary I want to tell you. The extraordinariness of it is enormous, maybe even more so than my virginity, because it's something that I would never reveal to just anyone. Apart from my dad, you're going to be the first guy to get a close-up of my being. Over the past three years, it has been this extraordinary thing that has mattered to me more than anything else. I had to trust first that if you discovered the truth, you'd still love me and care about me just as you always have.

Today, I feel wholly confident that you truly fathom the truth of what it means to be human. From what you've shown me, I'm convinced that you cherish every life. Even little insects with their measly lifespans, you have the heart to pity and treat with compassion. You never look down on anybody, never pick on anybody, never laugh at people who are more disadvantaged. You are a gentleman not only to me, you are a gentleman to every single thing on the face of the earth. So I'm confident that no matter who I am, no matter how different my constituent parts are from other people's, you wouldn't judge me based merely on my exterior shell. Because you understand the world. You understand that every life is born equal, each with a heart that beats to a similar rhythm, and each with a nose for inhaling air into the lungs alike. So what if I'm missing a tail? What difference does it make to the overall picture? Even if I'm a mock tail, I'm still me. I have faith you'll understand.)"

Reaching for the picture frame—her partner in conversation—Shamada drew it toward her face. Her smile in that moment was the image of serenity. She stared into the two-dimensional eyes of the man in the picture for a while before closing her eyes sweetly and then stamping her lips on the cold, clear slab.

Tomorrow her life was about to change, mentally and physically.

But in this instant, she felt like having another shower.

—

In a dorm room near the university campus, Komtal

was zonked out on top of his hefty schoolbook at his messy desk. He jumped back to his senses when his roommate Tupachet elbowed him, ramming these words into his ears: "Hey, let's watch some porn!"

True, it wasn't a particularly pretty or pleasing wake-up call, but it made Komtal straighten his back. "What are you on about?" he grumbled, rubbing his eyes.

"Here, look at this." Tupachet was waving a white-sleeved videotape—did he think it was a flag or something? "Finally, it's ours—almost the entire university's male student population have got their dirty hands on it. Plus, some kinky girls looking to satisfy their curiosity have secretly watched it, too! Tonight, at last, we're going to check out the freaky contents of this video. Let's see if it's as wild as it's rumored to be."

Having said his piece, Tupachet put the tape down on top of the TV receiver in the corner of the room. Then he walked over to the mini fridge and crouched down, opening it to look for a cold can of beer. He was in luck—there was a can hiding behind a plate of green mangoes, as if it had been waiting for him. Tupachet didn't waste any time—he snatched it, popped it open and took a gulp right away.

"What the hell's the movie?" Glancing down at the Russian history book spread open on his desk,

Komtal shook his head side to side thrice and then folded the two halves of the book together. Let's call it a day for now. I'll be studious again when I have time, he thought to himself.

"What?" Tupachet raised an eyebrow at his friend, all in good fun. He ran his hand over his hair, which had been sprayed rock-hard, before he continued: "You don't know what this video is? Oh! I risked my life fighting for it, wresting it away from a crowd at least ten strong so that the two of us could feast our eyes on the world-renowned picture that our male peers are currently buzzing about. It turns out my friend's been living under a goddamn rock, ignorant of my heroic deed and totally blind to the value of what I've managed to take possession of and am trying to bestow upon him."

Bending down, Komtal reached for the tangerine peels in the trash can next to the desk and flung them through the air, landing them on some part of his friend's face. Komtal himself didn't catch which part it was either, because the peels ricocheted upon impact and fell to the floor. "If you're going keep rambling on, how the fuck am I supposed to figure out what video it is?"

Tupachet knitted his eyebrows, letting it be known that Komtal's move displeased him. Why did he have

to go and throw something filthy at him?! "You… "
He wanted to swear at him but couldn't quite come
up with a word that hit the spot, so he backed down
and walked over to get the videotape, taking it in his
left hand, while his right hand continued to cradle the
beer can.

"Mock tail sex, dummy. Have you heard of that?"
Tupachet put the beer down in the spot previously
occupied by the tape and, using both hands, he pulled
the tape out of its sleeve, ready to slide the rectangular
cassette into the player under the base of the TV.

"Whoa, whoa, hold on! Don't turn it on yet. Can
you elaborate a bit more—what am I being forced to
watch?" With Komtal half yelling, Tupachet was com-
pelled to leave the cassette stuck in the VCR's mouth.

Aggravated, he let out a sigh, "Oh, oh, oh, my
friend." His tone was an obvious mix of mockery
and sarcasm. "It's porn similar to the sort that you
and I, sir, have purchased for our viewing pleasure,
the sort that we've watched until our eyes and our
something else turn red. Only this one has a special
weird feature, which is that all the lead actresses in this
movie are what you and I call 'mock tails.' Yes, sir, the
women with the beautiful faces and physiques that
you are about to see on the screen in front of you are
people who don't have these." Tupachet reached his

right hand around to fist the hose-shaped body part dangling behind him, rearranging it so as to have it poking next to his torso.

Once Komtal had digested his friend's explanation, he slapped himself on the forehead. "You perv! What do you want that sort of stuff for? I just want to kick back in peace."

"Hey, wasn't I telling you that practically the entire school has watched it? If I don't watch it, how am I supposed to be able to hobnob with the rest of society? C'mon, let's turn it on for a bit, just enough to get a sense of what it's like. Then I'll turn it off. From thereon in, if you want to kick back, lie back, sit back, stand back or do whatever you want to do to please or pleasure yourself, that's up to you." Tupachet turned back around and nudged the cassette in, letting the player suck it in the rest of the way—then he pushed play.

"Dick!" Komtal shouted, making sure that his collocutor got an earful.

Tupachet covertly stifled a grin. He was having a great time inflicting mental torture on his roommate.

Whoever it was who had last inspected the contents of this mock tail sex tape hadn't inspected it to the end and hadn't rewound it back to the beginning, because when Tupachet started the VCR's operation, the picture that naughtily popped up on-screen showed a no-holds-barred, indecent activity in the nude between a solidly built man and a slender young woman. The two actors didn't have to flip or slip into more creative positions before it became immediately apparent to Tupachet and Komtal that the naked girl was without a crucial body part. She was a human being who didn't possess the full set of thirty-three parts: the area above her buttocks was blank. It looked somehow odd, somehow weirdly bare—it was hard to describe. It was an image that normal people didn't get to see very often. She was definitely an authentic mock tail—there was no doubt about it.

Komtal couldn't stop himself from looking down to check on the well-being of his own tail. When he saw that all was in order, his mind was immediately put at ease.

Thank goodness I wasn't born a mock tail, he thought.

The phone rang. Because it was closer to Tupachet's hand, he scooched over to answer it.

"Your sweetheart," he handed the phone to his friend, after recognizing the voice. As Komtal reached his hand out to take the receiver, he signaled to Tupachet to turn down the volume on the moaning and groaning coming from the television set.

"Baby?" Komtal used a completely different tone from the one he'd used to communicate with his guy friend earlier, causing Tupachet to turn and grimace at him.

"What are you up to?" Shamada cooed over the line. In her head, she desperately wanted to tell her sweetheart the good news. She wanted to say: Komtal, baby, do you know what's about to happen tomorrow? I want to tell you, I want to confess my love to you. A whole bunch of words are jammed together at the tip of my tongue, so many of them that the entire thing feelth thwollen. I want to tell you everything all at once right this moment.

"I'd fallen asleep studying. Then all of a sudden Chet came into the room and yelled right in my ear, and now he's forcing me to sit through a gross movie and giving me no choice," Komtal recounted, deadpan, his eyes glued to the TV screen. He felt discombobulated by the female star's form and action, and it was making his stomach churn as if tiny waves from the sea had found themselves a new home in there and were curling inside. In front of the screen, Tupachet was whispering to himself: "Whoa! Strange but true!"

"What's the gross movie?" The voice on the line was still chipper.

She was waiting eagerly for Komtal's answer. No matter what he was about to say, that gentlemanly voice alone…

It was sure to make her swoon.

PART 6: NEW HAND

"Can I hold your hand?" Just last Saturday evening, the boy had gone to see a movie, and he'd picked up the line from a cutesy love scene.

The girl sat there awhile, charmed by the idea, before she gave her answer with enthusiasm: "Sure, take it."

She gave him her left hand.

He took it nervously.

And then the girl sprinted off, disappearing into the luscious glow of the evening sun, leaving the boy to sit there in a tangle of emotions, staring at the third hand he held in his right hand. No one had ever given him their hand so nonchalantly before. Happy? Sure, he could say he was happy, because he'd had a secret crush on the girl for months. Being in possession of her hand surely meant that he'd managed to chisel away a few layers of brick from the wall separating their personal spaces.

But the happiness dissipated in no time, replaced instead by anxiety.

He didn't know how to behave toward the girl's hand now that he had it.

As the dusky sky set in, the boy decided to go home.

"Hurry up and have a shower, sweetie. I've got dinner ready," his mother caught sight of him coming in just after she heard the front door shut. She was standing in the kitchen, peeling yellow-fleshed oranges. Her eyes toggled back and forth very quickly from her son to the fruit, but she was eagle-eyed enough to spot the foreign object in his hand. She immediately did a double take, turning her head with a whoosh. "And whose hand have you got there, huh?"

"A friend from school's, Mom." Although his account was not precisely truthful, it didn't quite fall under the category of a lie either. But when he added out of nervousness that "sh—he lent it to me", well, now he was toeing a mighty fine line between sin and innocence.

Footsteps could be heard descending the stairs as the boy peeled a dark-brown school sock off the end of his left foot. The trampling march belonged to none other than his sister. Because she was home, she was dressed casually: eye-catching hot pants in dark blue, a white tank top in a fabric so thin that no eye-straining was required to see through it, both pieces of clothing hugging her body tight.

"Mom!" she yelled all the way to the back of the kitchen seconds after she'd made her way down. "Mom!" she yelled again, stressing her demand.

"What, honey? Can you not make so much noise?" Their mother tossed out those words, along with the tough green rind of one of the oranges. She wondered how this daughter of hers started exhibiting the loudness inherited from her maternal grandfather, and at such a young age? She was still really just becoming a woman. She shouldn't have any reason to shout with her mouth wide open the way she did on a regular basis.

"Who left whose hand on the table?" His sister was still screaming at the top of her lungs as she grabbed the mystery hand from the marble table and flipped it around for inspection.

Once the boy realized what had ignited his sister's curiosity, he nearly sprained his neck jerking his head around in an effort to make an urgent assessment of the situation. Upon seeing the delicate hand being touched in that manner, without authorization, he immediately charged in to protect the new object under his care.

"Your brother said his friend lent it to him," their mother answered through the kitchen door.

"A female friend, too. The skin's nice and smooth." His sister yanked the hand out of his lunging range. At the corners of her mouth, a little smile sprouted. It was a smile of satisfaction from being able to taunt her baby brother, who was smaller and powerless to retaliate.

"Give it back!" the boy screamed, his voice filling the room. His hands were swinging and swatting the air in front of him as he tried to claw his way to the object in his sister's hand. "Give it back to me. It's mine. You're going to bruise it!" The more he struggled and scrambled, the more hopeless the situation became for him. The span of his sister's arm, combined with the stretch of her teen girl torso, created a predicament. No matter how much he redoubled his efforts at grabbing and grappling, he was like a dog jumping at the sky, dreaming of grasping the moon.

"Mom! Mom! Mom! Mom! Mom!" The boy turned and fired his voice into the kitchen as if he were a gunman pumping bullets.

Every shot had hit their mother's nerves, forcing her to shout back to ease the pain of her wounds. "What is it now, you two siblings!"

"Mom! She won't give the hand back to me." The

boy was on edge. A hint of sniveling appeared as he strained to get his words out.

Tormenting him was a distinct source of amusement for his sister. She was beaming; the budding smile on her face had now bloomed into a wide grin infected with laughter. The girl's hand was tossed back and forth—left here, right there—evading the boy's pursuit—the boy, hot on his sister's heels. Meanwhile, she started to move along the edge of the table. Now the two were tangled together like an acrobatics duo.

"First tell me whose hand this is! What's her name? Which homeroom is she in? What does she look like? Is she your girlfriend?" his sister asked over the sound of his attempts to tackle her midair.

"Mom! Mom! Mom! Mom! Mom!" The boy fired off another round, even though his mother's ears were still bleeding from the previous bullets.

"Stop making so much noise! Give the hand back to your brother! And get ready to eat dinner already. Go get your dad. He's probably still outside washing the car."

The sister made no move to execute the command from the kitchen.

"Mom! She won't quit picking on me," the boy groaned, fishing for sympathy. Worn out, he was relinquishing his attempt to keep up the struggle using his own physical strength. He stood in place and stared at his sister, his face boiling with rage.

Seeing him scowl, his sister gloated even more. She couldn't resist provoking him further, even though in her heart she felt nothing but fondness for him. She bullied him out of love—the impulse was a complex one. The more despondent the look she detected in her brother's eyes, the more she felt the enormity of her influence over him. The more she was able to ruffle his feathers, the deeper their relationship seemed to her. When I'm nice to the kid, he can't even be bothered looking my way, she thought.

"Go get Dad first, and then I'll give it back," she laid out her condition as she raised one eyebrow and squinted the opposite eye, appearing not at all trustworthy.

"Mom! She won't give my friend's hand back." Even though the boy's gaze was latched on his sister's face, his words were again directed at his mother in the kitchen.

"I told him to go get Dad for dinner first, and then I'll give it back, Mom, really," his sister explained the supposedly mutual agreement which she had in fact concocted on her own.

Their mother shook her head wearily, her eyes still focused on an orange, the seventh one. As for the seeds she was carving out of its yellow flesh, she hadn't kept count of how many there'd been. Why does family life have to be so full of such nonsense? Every day there's something to cause a headache and an earache. Each episode just materializes, without the conduct of human life necessitating any of it. This pair of siblings never makes an effort to learn to live together in peace. Is there any rhyme or reason as to why they must chase each other around the dinner table, tussling over someone else's hand? No, there's no rhyme, there's no reason, but somehow these incidents have become routine in this household.

"Promise your brother first—and keep your promise." She tried to iron out a situation she hadn't wrinkled; that was one of the items in a housewife's job description, one on par with peeling oranges.

His sister brandished a victor's smirk. "I promise I'll give you your girlfriend's hand back once you go out and get Dad," she said, and then held the hand above her head, waving it around in her own right hand.

The boy found it incredulous that his mother would side with his sister to such a degree. Was it possible that due to their common sex as females, they ultimately shared a female logic? "Hruumph," he made his dissatisfaction known by hacking his emotion up his windpipe and followed up with some light foot-stomping.

But "your girlfriend's hand": these three words from his sister's mouth tickled him. Deep down, he was secretly hoping that they would become reality in the not-so-distant future. Who knows... that future might be tomorrow, after some cozy alone time with the girl's hand this evening.

"You have to keep your promise," he said sullenly, before he opened the front door and stepped into the garage, tracking his father by the sound of his whistled song. Somewhere, a cat meowed in a lonesome tenor, probably a gray cat, given the scant light that remained.

"Is everything alright, son?" His father broke off the melody he was making with his lips as he looked up from the water that formed an arc shooting out of his green hose en route to plopping against the shiny silver surface of his car. "What's with the sour face?"

"Mom told me to come get you for dinner." The boy tried to avoid answering the question directly, but the angle of his chin was a dead giveaway of his distress.

His father dropped the hose on the ground, letting the water run and collect into a puddle as he walked over to the tap to stop the flow. "Did you get into an argument with someone, huh?" Sometimes his father could read him like an open book. "What did your sister do to you this time?"—so stunningly like a book that when the boy lifted his chin so his face was vertical, his irises might as well have been exclamation marks!

"She took something of mine and won't give it back," he divulged. "She said she'd only give it back if I came out and got you first."

His father coiled up the hose and hung the loop on the neck of the tap. "What did she take?" Making his way around, he picked up the car-washing supplies that were scattered about on the cement floor. Two sponges lay soaked to capacity. His father picked one up and squeezed it dry.

Embarrassed, the boy hesitated, deliberating. He didn't often discuss girls with his father. "A friend's hand," he let his answer drop quietly.

His father tossed the second sponge—now already wrung dry—into a tin can next to the tap where the first sponge lay waiting. 'A friend's hand'; he replayed his son's words back and forth in the parts of his brain by his temples, and then he pressed further in good humor. "Hmm, as far as I can remember, you've never brought a friend's hand home before. Is there something special about it, huh?" He turned to give his son a sly smile. He knows again?

"The hand," the boy clammed up despite having done nothing wrong. "The. Hand. Belongs. To. A. Girl." By the time he got all the words out of his mouth, the boy had let slip a window of opportunity where his guard was down, and his father made the most of the time by picking up all the rags and towels from different areas on the ground.

"Oh!" His father chuckled, finding the scenario endearing. "A lady's hand." With his supplies now properly stowed away, he turned the water on again to wash his hands. "My son's becoming a man, isn't he? Alright, good, good. Soon, us father and son will be able to consult each other on this sort of thing in more intimate detail," he said, sounding chipper, and then he laughed.

The boy looked on as his father squatted and cupped water in his hands. He had no clue what sort of thing his father was referring to, but it sounded sort of nice to have him around to help sort out an assortment of questions—if he needed to resort to that.

"Dad," the boy started soliciting advice from his father straight away. "What does it mean when a girl lets you take her hand home like this? What are the things I should do with the hand?"

His father stood over the tap, watching a few sputtering drops splatter onto the ground. Putting his wet hands on the seat of his shorts, he tossed two kinds of tissue—skin and cloth—together, distributing the moisture as he stepped toward his son, who had been standing in the same spot the entire time.

"My boy." He embraced his son's shoulders. "When a woman lets you take her hand with you, first, it means she's starting to trust you, starting to want to risk it with you. She does it as a test to see how well a man might take care of her hand. Therefore, if you like this girl, you have to cherish her hand, you have to wash and bathe it, wipe and scrub it nicely. Because the following day is the day the girl will decide how she feels about you. If you return her hand in good condition, then she'll know that you really care about her. Do you understand?" The boy nodded, although he wasn't entirely sure yet if he did.

That was a sign of being a man: whatever the situation, nod firmly, even if you're in the dark.

"When you were a kid, did you take a girl's hand home very often?" The boy was curious.

His father pressed his index finger to his lips, his face lit up with glee. "Shhhh, we have to be quiet. Otherwise you mother might hear us." The boy laughed. "When I was a kid? I don't want to brag. Some days I got several. You could say, I could hardly handle them all," his father told him, mimicking an elaborate act of a juggler. "But," he suddenly sounded serious, "in the end, your mother's hand was the one I found myself wanting to cherish the most, so the other girls' hands no longer meant anything. That's what's important—you have to learn to tell whose hand is the one dearest to you, and then you have to cling to it so that you have it by your side forever."

Then his father pushed through the front door, steering his son into the house as well.

Once inside, the boy surveyed the room with his eyes: there was no sign of the hand or of his pain-in-the-butt sister. He freed himself from his father's arm and ran toward the doorway to the kitchen.

His mother and sister were standing side by side. When they heard his footsteps approach, the two turned to look at him in unison, apprehension written all over their faces.

"Sis, I got Dad. Where's my friend's hand?" Before he received an answer, his eyes fell on the familiar object, lying inert by the pile of orange peels on the wooden tabletop in front of his mother and sister.

On the girl's delicate, creamy-soft hand appeared a bright red spot at the tip of the thumb.

"Sweetie," his mother sounded skittish. "Your sister didn't mean to."

"I accidentally dropped it, and it got nicked by the point of Mom's knife. It's only a little cut. I'll put iodine on it and dress it for you." His sister's rambunc-tiousness had completely vanished, and her face was full of remorse.

The hand had been cut by a knife! How was this supposed to be considered proper care and pamper-ing? Would the girl be willing to forgive him? What woman was ever going to give him her hand again in this life?

The boy rushed to the hand, seized it and cra-dled it, tears bursting out of his eyes as if a dam had exploded. His mother and sister looked at each other helplessly, at a loss as to how to comfort him.

They left him alone to cry over a girl's hand for the first time in his young life.

He hugged the wounded hand tight, bolted out of the kitchen, tears and all, and leapt up the stairs to his room on the second floor.

Door slammed shut, he made a beeline for the bathroom, turned on the faucet and placed the girl's hand in the sink, positioning it under the clear stream of water to rinse off the blood effectively.

Then at the sudden urge of his flustered head, he stepped away to pick up the phone and call his pal in order to vent. As he walked off, the sound of water plopping against the flesh of the hand pursued him, echoing in his head.

"What the hell happened?" The boy had sniveled into the receiver as soon as he'd heard his friend's hello. "My sister caused a big mess."

"Hey! Can I call you back in an hour? I'm kind of busy right now," his friend pleaded.

"What are you busy doing?" The boy's feelings were hurt, and his voice made it abundantly clear. It stung him that even his dear friend couldn't spare a moment for him during a critical time like this.

"I'm taking care of a girl's hand. This one happens to be cute, too. I'm in the middle of grooming her nails," the friend explained.

"Whose is it, the one you say's cute?" the boy interrogated, peeved.

Once his friend spoke her name, the boy felt stiff as numbness swamped his whole body.

Her name was the same one that belonged to the owner of the hand in the sink, the hand that had been cut by a knife.

He'd got her left hand; his friend her right.

Instead of questioning what kind of girl would give her hands to two different guys on the same day, he broke into an anxious sweat.

"How on earth is she going to choose me?"

The boy—he was a new hand at this sort of thing.

PART 7: BELLY UP

He picked up the nickname 'Mantique from his friends during his time at university.

Because among the guys in his faculty—all rather busted-looking—he was hailed as the most romantic.

Because he already had the nickname Man.

Because he didn't like the nickname his father had given him and preferred to style himself more femininely as Tooktique.

Because Man was romantic, because Man was Tooktique, because Tooktique said flamboyant, because flamboyant said femme, because he was she.

Thus, Man was 'Mantique to her friends.

She was proud of the moniker and fully embraced it when referring to herself.

"'Mantique thinks… ," she often started a conversation that way, using her name as the first-person pronoun, because every sound that found its way out of her mouth really communicated 'Mantique's thoughts, not Man's, not those of Apichart Piangwang—the full name on her national ID card. Whenever anyone asked, "'Mantique, what's your real name, missy?" the question tended to make her head do a prissy little spin, because it wounded her feelings, being suddenly reminded that her true name was Apichart.

What is true, what is false, what is real, what is fake? For 'Mantique, 'Mantique's real name is just 'Mantique. As for that Mr. Apichart, that was a technical error, a flub on the part of 'Mantique's parents who got frisky before they knew better. But ultimately, the one who's going to write the script of 'Mantique's life is 'Mantique, that's what 'Mantique thinks.

"My real name is Ro-man-tique, darling."

—

'Mantique thought today at sunrise would be a good time to kill herself.

Each to their own perspective. Some people look down on suicide as a cowardly choice, as an easy and irresponsible way to escape problems. In Thai, a euphemism for suicide is "shortsighted thinking"… but 'Mantique thinks you should give credit to people who have the guts to really carry it through all the way to the end. Us mortals, we're usually afraid to death of getting hurt. To get themselves to the point of jabbing, stabbing, hacking, slicing or shooting at their own flesh, people need steely resolve, the resolve to go through with it once and for all (or more than once if they don't quite die. Hahaha!).

'Mantique thinks 'Mantique's jealous of these people, because 'Mantique's not decisive, 'Mantique's half-brave, half-skittish, half-dreaming, half-doing, half-this and half-that, but 'Mantique never "goes ahead with it," as they say in English. Because of this, no one believes in 'Mantique, no one loves 'Mantique for real. They dupe 'Mantique then dump 'Mantique, then dupe then dump, like that, over and over. 'Mantique's no piece of trash. Ah! Ah! Don't dump 'Mantique—the Magic Eyes of the trash campaign see you!

'Mantique's sick of 'Mantique's own inadequacy, sick of having to be lonesome again for the umpteenth time, sick of the tiny little rented room that doesn't have a chic vanity table, sick of the nocturnal life that leaves 'Mantique's under-eyes puffy... So, this morning, 'Mantique thinks 'Mantique's going to commit suicide.

Eeeek! But the thought of stabbing 'Mantique's own plump and tender organs with a sharp object, 'Mantique can't, darling. The idea makes 'Mantique shudder. Pouring drugs down 'Mantique's own throat, that's not 'Mantique's strong suit either. 'Mantique has a history of allergies to too many kinds of medication, and 'Mantique doesn't like how they taste. So, after sitting down and mulling it over, 'Mantique thinks 'Mantique's more suited to jumping from a great height. By the time the blood spills and splashes and splatters, 'Mantique won't be around to witness it any longer. It seems like a more pleasant way to go.

Once the method was chosen, 'Mantique jumped right on it, darling, dashing upstairs to reserve the rooftop of the apartment building for the occasion. In a million years, 'Mantique had never graced it with 'Mantique's presence, no. It's a filthy place. Late at night, often there are teenagers sitting around in a group up there, drinking and keeping themselves entertained with dirty tales. It's a cross between terrifying and disgusting, a combination that's just too intense and probably very dangerous for a prim and pretty person like 'Mantique. So 'Mantique had always refrained from wandering up there, for the peace and prosperity of all involved. But this morning, 'Mantique was on a special mission that necessitated the climb.

Let 'Mantique tell you about it... It can count as 'Mantique's daily dose of humor.

'Mantique went up there and stood awkwardly on top of the cement parapet on the rooftop, peeking down at the concrete surface of the road below. Because it was still early and the sun hadn't entirely detached itself from the horizon yet, mosquitoes swarmed and swooped all over the place. Upon seeing 'Mantique's gorgeous skin, they probably felt peckish, so the whole horde of them started biting and nibbling along the entire lengths of 'Mantique's arms in a feeding frenzy. It bugged 'Mantique, even though 'Mantique was just about to jump off the side of the building toward death. But 'Mantique couldn't stand it and had to spare almost forty minutes swatting the mosquitoes. Darling, 'Mantique had a fortress set up to fight off the enemies. 'Mantique stood there, slapping, intent on eradicating them all. There were over a hundred dead bodies before 'Mantique was finished. Hands all smudged with tiny little bloodstains, 'Mantique was worried about ruining 'Mantique's fine skin, so 'Mantique had to run back to the room and wash the grossness off and rub moisturizer on after. Once that task was accomplished, 'Mantique went up the stairs again, intending to face death once more.

Too late! Not the time of day, darling, because it wasn't quite 7:00 a.m. yet then. The air was still fresh, with the moist scent of morning dew period-ically grazing the nose. The elements of dawn were all there. But it was too late because when 'Mantique craned 'Mantique's neck to look down for the sec-ond time at the ground below—gray, trimmed with white-ish, yellow-ish lines—the fear of pain poked up in 'Mantique's bosom. 'Mantique was thinking, that's concrete, darling self. That's no cotton wool, no sili-cone, no waterbed, no bouncy rubber, no velvet, no wool—that's something really hard, like, painful-hard, hard enough to crack your bones in the blink of an eye, and it's not the kind of hard 'Mantique likes either. No, thank you. 'Mantique thinks it's too cruel, it's not romantic. 'Mantique thinks a person like 'Mantique should at least get to go in a tasteful and graceful manner, like a well-composed painting that possesses elegance, that's moving, that conveys death in the abstract.

'Mantique thought a change of plans might be better: to die by jumping off a bridge.

Because that would be a true return to one of the four elements of life, a romantic separation from the earth, 'Mantique-style.

'Mantique thinks 'Mantique should get dressed, flag a taxi in front of the building, and tell the driver to step on it to get to the Suspension Bridge before 7:30.

And so she did just that. At the foot of the bridge on the Bangkok side, when 'Mantique shut the door of the pink-and-white taxi behind her, most people's clocks and watches read 7:23. 'Mantique thought she had correctly estimated the time, but she had no way of knowing for sure because she had decided not to put on a watch before leaving home, and the clock in the taxi was defective. For upward of a month, it had said that the time was 4:36, that was what the driver told her. Only we know that 'Mantique had arrived at her destination a good several minutes ahead of schedule.

Walking up the curve of the bridge, 'Mantique didn't even so much as glance at the water flowing alongside her below because she didn't want to lock eyes with her own graveyard before the necessary moment.

But then the necessary moment caught up to her fast, at the bridge's midway point. 'Mantique thought the coldness of the water she saw below was probably no laughing matter. She clenched both fists, as if doing so were a means of gathering the strength she needed to jump, ignorant of the fact that hardly any physical power was required. Really, what 'Mantique should have been gathering were memories, those that might have been hiding deep within or fallen through the cracks in the nooks of her brain or the crannies of her heart, the good and the bad, the beautiful and the battered, the memorable and the forgettable.

Had 'Mantique ever wondered why memories which deserve to be forgotten to keep flaunting themselves, taunting us, enduring with greater sharpness and clarity than the ones that deserve safekeeping? Because even though it's impossible, deep down everybody hopes to have a chance to do over something that won't stop gnawing at us. Even though it's unrealistic, everybody wants to have a giant eraser hidden inside of them that they can pull out and use whenever they make a blunder.

They say memories are like scars. 'Mantique doesn't like scars. 'Mantique wonders why these so-called living wounds must stay alive. An entire person has to cease to exist in order for these permanent marks to give up their existence. 'Mantique thinks it's such a waste of a life. But that's that. What can you do if it's the only way?

'Mantique thought she should have her eyes closed when she stepped off and let herself fall from life, so she wouldn't have to witness the vertical rush of the world zooming by. 'Mantique thought she might throw up otherwise.

The second she threw her body over, what was

going through her mind?

'Mantique thought her body might get nibbled on by fish in the near future. What an unpalatable image.

Layers of air never helped buoy anyone up. Quivers ran through her whole body, as if the soles of her feet had holes allowing air to enter and squirm inside of her, forcing blood cells of both colors to become jammed at her temples. 'Mantique couldn't think anymore.

Then, before she hit the surface of the water, her body started to fall more slowly, which she found rather strange. 'Mantique still didn't dare peel her eyes open, fearing that she would see something unpleasant, like a reddish liquid or some roundish gobs sticky with mucus.

But 'Mantique's curious bone couldn't resist. 'Mantique's thinking, what's happening here? Suddenly, the belly feels bloated and stretched taut, as if it's struggling to push something out, as though it's slowly inflating like a balloon—yes, like a balloon with an air pump sticking into it. But there's nothing sticking into 'Mantique. There's only air that's going by in the reverse direction, but that shouldn't be spiky enough to pierce the body and make it expand. 'Mantique thinks it's time to inspect the situation with 'Mantique's own eyes and see what's going on with 'Mantique's svelte body.

Aaah! 'Mantique's belly is puffed up as round as a ball. It's ripped to shreds the trusty T-shirt that was meant to be taken along on 'Mantique's tour of the next world, and now 'Mantique's outie belly button is exposed, looking oddly like the stem-end on a fruit. And 'Mantique feels, too, that instead of dropping further down and into the water according to plan, 'Mantique's inflated belly is buoying up 'Mantique's body, preventing it from falling with the motion of gravity. If that isn't strange enough, it's now gradually shooing 'Mantique back upward, encouraging 'Mantique to float exactly like a balloon. Or is hell turning 'Mantique away? Or perhaps 'Mantique's extreme romanticism is better suited for angels than for the Guardian of Hell?

There's nothing 'Mantique can do. 'Mantique is floating up higher and higher. 'Mantique wonders whether anyone on the streets below notices this miracle. 'Mantique thinks it would be good to try flapping 'Mantique's arms, just for kicks, so 'Mantique looks more elegant, so it looks as if 'Mantique were the one directing this upward movement. Otherwise people will think 'Mantique swallowed a cheap balloon from a temple fair into the belly—that doesn't sound romantic at all. 'Mantique's flapping 'Mantique's arms, pretending they're wings of a bird. If 'Mantique flashes a little smile, it'd probably look like 'Mantique's having a good time flying.

Hey you, Suspension Bridge, we're at the same level again. 'Mantique didn't think we'd ever meet again. Oh, whoa! Bye, Bridge, 'Mantique's belly is so impatient. Is it in a rush to shoot up and go explore Mars or what? The higher it's getting, the more speed it's picking up. This is freaky in a different way. Good thing 'Mantique's not afraid of a little height (not just not afraid, loves it even. 'Mantique likes them tall and fair. Hahaha!). 'Mantique's never been on an airplane. 'Mantique's only heard people talk about how, from the window, everything below looks tiny like toys, like Barbie's stuff. 'Mantique's getting a pretty good sense of that firsthand now, and 'Mantique's liking it.

Reflections on the surface of the water look so beautiful from here. The orange sunlight is skimming the raised bits of the water section by section—'Mantique's not describing it well because 'Mantique's not gifted at using words nicely to describe an image in a way that tugs at people's heartstrings. But 'Mantique likes to try because 'Mantique likes to read touching poems. Reading them gives 'Mantique the feeling that something nice-smelling is blooming under the eyelids. What's happening to 'Mantique now lends itself to being turned into beautiful phrases, but sadly 'Mantique can probably only do what 'Mantique's abilities will allow. If 'Mantique floats past a S.E.A. Write poet's window, 'Mantique will drag him out and ask him to help compose a poem, but probably no S.E.A. Write poet's awake yet.

Where is 'Mantique floating to? It's starting to get higher and higher. Ahhh! Real birds! A whole flock of them. Give a little way, pretty, please. Phew! Even in the open sky, you can still run into things that make your heart race.

Why didn't 'Mantique die, even though 'Mantique was dying to? What's happening to 'Mantique's belly? What sneaky thing has wiggled its way in there? Or has it had these parachute-like qualities from the time 'Mantique's eyes opened to see the world for the first time? 'Mantique doesn't recall being aware of this. Or is 'Mantique pregnant! That's going a bit overboard. Even if pregnancy were a possibility, it's unlikely that it would be so lightning-fast. In sum, 'Mantique thinks it's impossible to know the real reason why the belly inflated...

—

"Hey, isn't that Man?" Mrs Urai Piangwang flinched when she saw a round-bellied human floating in the bit of sky outside her window.

"Don't utter that name within my earshot," Mr. Apichai Piangwang doggedly kept his eyes on his newspaper, his right hand holding a plastic coffee mug by the handle.

"But—our Man is floating in the sky with his belly puffed up. Look!" Her voice was animated and concerned. When she became certain that what she saw before her eyes was her only son, she was even made to slide the sash window up (and it was a window that hadn't been washed or opened for years) and stick her head out to get a good look. "Man! Man! Man, my son!" She yelled into the morning air.

"Don't bother with him. It's his business what he's up to. Since he doesn't care about our feelings, why should we care about him?" There was so much bitterness in Mr. Apichai's tone that he was gagging on it. Whenever his wife mentioned their son's name, he inevitably gave the same speech, as if he had it memorized. The wound in his heart had never begun to heal, no matter that a whole forest's worth of trees had perished in the meantime in the form of torn-off calendar pages.

"But—our son's floating in the air! He's not just walking by the house. Aren't you going to look? How the heck did he get himself into this?" Mrs. Urai turned to say to her husband and then quickly slipped her head back out, tilting her face toward the sky. "Man! Man! Can you hear your mother?"

"That's not out of character for him, these wacky, weird things. He just loves to seek out outlandish things to amuse himself with, absurdly going off and doing this and that. Any moral compass he ever had was shattered to pieces long ago. We're lucky he isn't living here with us anymore. Otherwise we'd embarrass ourselves all the way from here down the whole street." Mr. Apichai cleared his throat as if to hack out a ball of pain.

"Man!" Mrs. Urai tried again.

This time, 'Mantique happened to be looking her way.

'Mantique thinks the little woman at the window over there looks familiar. Aaahh! It's 'Mantique's own mother! 'Mantique hasn't seen her for ages. Must wave hello before the belly takes 'Mantique floating up too far for us to see each other.

'Mantique frantically waved her right hand again and again.

"Hey! Man's waving to us!" Mrs Urai shrieked with joy.

"So what!" Mr. Apichai said, teeth gritted.

But he took a peek out of the corner of his eye.

The hole in his heart had never closed up…

PART 8: A HAIRY SITUATION

A lot of people love theirs... to the point of infatuation.

If anyone were to touch or mess with theirs, the transgression wouldn't be an easy matter to brush off.

The level of attachment, devotion, and fixation is so peculiar that it deserves to be recorded somewhere on the face of the earth for preservation in the event that intelligent humans of the future are able to use the information to advance the research on human genetics.

We're talking about... hair. It's something that can grow back, unless nature has condemned certain areas of a person's scalp to exist as barren land, forever hairless. Some are doomed to this fate, driven to anguish by the sparseness that appears sketchy at best, no matter how they try to cover it up; they can't ever make it look as elegant as the real thing.

But for others—and the head count here's not so

low—their hair is thick and voluminous, as it should be. Even if it were to be clipped off with grass shears, or sliced off with a surgeon's knife from the emergency room, or plucked out with giant tweezers, before long the strands would sprout back, poking and prickling through the follicles that lie flat on the scalp, and bloom back in full bunches, returning to their former silky splendor.

Why then do so many people have to guard their hairdos so jealously, lest their faces alter? An obvious example are the many guys endowed with a healthy dose of artistic sensibility, who prefer to keep their hair long and flowing, so the plush messiness framing their faces can help maintain some semblance of an introspective nature. No way I'd let anyone chop mine off! Some even refuse to apply for employment at a workplace where hair must be worn short. They would rather bite the bullet and live on a dime a day to preserve the pulchritude of their coiffures which swish and sway with each flutter of the wind. The resolve with which these image-conscious men hold on to their principle is truly admirable.

Some ladies aren't to be outdone, maintaining their hair to the lengths where gravity has it hanging down to their butt cheeks. If they're not on guard, their hair might get caught in a door—multiple times a day, or it might become a repository for bits of dried leaves, candy, chewing gum, or even bird poo, without their realizing it. But determination trumps all in life. I want to keep it long—who's going to say what? It doesn't weigh on anyone's head but mine.

This report concerns two people who reach a tie in their love for their hair.

One is male; the other is female.

One is a teacher; the other is a student.

One is twenty-five years old; the other is sixteen.

One has a car; the other does not, and does not yet know how to drive.

One is named Pravit; the other, Lila.

It was almost dusk but the sky was still light. School had been out for hours. Lila was sitting in Pravit's car, still in her school uniform, her hands clasped and resting in the dip of her skirt between her thighs. Her schoolbag was leaning against a small yellow pillow in the backseat. In the bag were her schoolbooks and notebooks, a pack of sanitary pads, and a purple plastic pencil case, which contained no pencils but three pens—one blue, one red, and one black; a round ink eraser; and two bobby pins. A third bobby pin was currently clipped on her head. Lila's hair, which fell all the way to the small of her back, was at that moment flattened between the body of its owner and the back of the seat, which smelled of old leather.

Mr. Pravit, the international-music teacher, was driving. His eyes were on the traffic ahead, looking through the lenses of his round silver-framed eyeglasses resting on the bridge of his nose. A motorbike swooped by on his side, squeezing in so close that it nearly swiped off the car's side-view mirror, and on top of that, its souped-up engine left a parting gift in the form of a deafening growl that continued to grate on the nerves for several minutes after.

Mr. Pravit was wearing a white button-down, khaki pants and black synthetic leather shoes that hadn't cost more than a few hundred baht. The shoes were a graduation present from his girlfriend, Jai. In his shirt pocket, he had a green rubber band lying flat against a twenty-baht bill. Mr. Pravit actually had two rubber bands, but the other one was tied around his long, disheveled hair to make it look tidier, more fitting for his position as a teacher, which he had held for several months.

The traffic was slow... Mr. Pravit took his eyes off the road and turned to consider the figure next to him. He could look at Lila's hair an infinite number of times, and he would never tire of it. Because of its length, it stood out from how the other high school girls wore theirs. At some schools, it was against the rules for girls to wear their hair that long. But that wasn't the only striking thing about Lila: precocious in all her proportions, she had the voluptuousness that left no doubt that hers was the physique of a woman. Her sharp features, too, caught every eye that happened upon them; they certainly caught his, immediately, on the first day he started working at the school.

"Lila," that was her name, someone had told him, unprompted. You could say she was the school's queen bee. The younger kids admired and idolized her; they wanted to be pretty and have beautiful eyes like Pi Lila. The older students—both the boys and the tomboys—had crushes on her, wanted to be at her service. They wanted to help her comb her mesmerizing long hair, the whole head, strand by strand..

"Lila," he'd repeated it slowly to himself after they'd first met—what a curiously melodious name. And when he got to say it out loud, it was even more of a tongue teaser and pleaser: there was no double consonant required, no tongue roll, nothing in his oral cavity was harmed in the pronouncing of it. It was easy to sound out but tuneful, like music notes (Do-Re-Mi-Fa-So-Lila-Ti-Do); the ears wanted to hear it, and the mouth wanted to say it again and again.

"Lila." They were still stuck in traffic, and Pravit's eyes were still stuck on that note, so he moved his lips, letting the lovely sound of her name swirl in the wind of his tongue.

"Yes?" Lila turned toward the voice, her tone delivering a question mark.

"If someone asked to buy your hair, would you sell it?" Mr. Pravit didn't simply speak, he also took the liberty of reaching his left hand out and gently stroking the comely Lila's precious prized possession. Gentleness—that was a quality of Mr. Pravit's which caused many of his female students to go weak in the knees: he made for the perfect picture of a dream gentleman, his eyes exuding a tender sensibility that wasn't quite flimsy but just right. Moreover, he had cascading long hair that could be caressed and braided for fun. There weren't many male teachers at the school who were so young, so laid-back, so sensitive in nature, and with hair so long. Compared to the other male teachers, Mr. Pravit was like Prince Charming in a castle, the object of desire for girls all over the kingdom—even fellow teachers.

Hearing the question, Lila giggled. "For how much?"

"Let's say, five thousand baht." Mr. Pravit withdrew his hand, replacing it on the steering wheel.

Several of the cars in front had started to roll forward.

The giggling stopped as Lila kept the sound of her amusement stuffed in the pockets of her cheeks, making them bubble out big and round. "Isn't that too little? If I'm going to go so far as to cut my hair and sell it, it's got to be for a good amount of money—worth the years of growing it out."

Mr. Pravit tapped the gas pedal with his foot. "Let's say, thirty thousand—there!" He punched up his words, having found his student's business rationale endearing. "Would you take thirty thousand?"

Lila went quiet for moment. "I think it's still too little. It's not worth it. It should be a bit more than that," she replied, and then she shifted a portion of her hair to the front, inspecting it to assess its value. "It took almost ten years to grow it this long," she said, beaming with pride.

"So how much? Fifty thousand? That's already halfway to six figures."

Lila hummed as she mulled it over, still unable to decide on a price that would be worth parting with a piece of her physical beauty for. As she was thinking about it, her mind wandered in another direction—perhaps it turned left like the steering wheel in Mr. Pravit's hands—and it prompted her to ask offhandedly: "And you? What price would you set for your hair?"

The young teacher had never considered the question. He held off on answering until the car had finished turning the curve and was on a straight course again.

"But my hair's not as beautiful as yours. Their values probably can't be compared."

This time the student was the one to reach her hand out and touch the teacher's jet-black hair, going for his squirrel tail. She caressed it with just a single stroke of the hand, but that single stroke made the young man tense up with excitement for several beats of his heart.

"True," Lila agreed in jest. "Not as beautiful as mine at all. But it's very long, too. Having grown it this long, surely you've got to be somewhat attached to it. You probably wouldn't sell it to anyone cheaply." A little pause. "Right?"

Through Lila's "Right?" Mr. Pravit could feel her round eyes fixed on him. Behind his glasses, his own eyes were taken up with the task of steering the car and couldn't fully take stock of the action around him. But the feeling was so ferocious and fiery that he immediately had to turn and look to be sure he wasn't imagining it.

Lila really was staring at him.

"So how much?" It was as if those words were delivered to him by the sheer force of her eyes.

Mr. Pravit felt hot and bothered. The roof of his mouth felt as though it had been contaminated with a strange substance that was unsettling his saliva. He lowered his gaze down to Lila's lap and saw that she still had one of her hands resting there, but it wasn't simply resting: the five fingers appeared to be moving up and down slowly as if they were tapping on a piano keyboard, making heavenly music for the world.

What's the song? What's the song? What's the song? Mr. Pravit asked himself in rapid fire, thinking the questions out in full, instead of economizing with the Thai symbol for repetition.

What song was she playing that had him enchanted?

"What's going on with you? Aren't you afraid of getting into an accident?" Lila pointed through the windshield—the melody was immediately cut off. Mr. Pravit jumped and immediately spun his head back toward the traffic.

"So? How much would you sell it for? Would you sell it for fifty thousand?"

"It depends on how much you'd sell yours for. Mine would probably be half that price. If you'd be willing to sell your hair for fifty thousand baht, then I'd sell for twenty-five thousand or so. Does that sound about right?" He cracked a smile to deflect his embarrassment. He felt ridiculous that he had allowed himself to daydream just because the darkest part of his imagination had been lightly tapped.

"But I probably wouldn't sell my hair. Except if I really needed the money. Getting it to this length again wouldn't be very easy."

Not easy, but not difficult either. All she needed was time.

"Why do you keep your hair long?" Lila was looking out at the street again, but her hands were busy pulling the bobby pin out of her hair. "Is it because you want to be an artist?"

She'd already answered for him in full. The reason had nothing more to it. He had an image in his head of what an artist looked like, and that was what he wanted to achieve, so he'd taken it upon himself to inspect the details on his own person. He's done whatever he could do to make himself similar or identical to that image. On his first day on campus at university, he'd decided to leave his hair and simply let it naturally grow long, occasionally trimming the ends but generally maintaining the style. Eventually, he became a long-haired guy as he had wished.

But for him to admit what she'd said was already correct felt somehow... Reasons can always be invented and embellished ex post. And if you set your sights on being a teacher, you have to learn to stock up on credible reasons—starting from the time you're still in teacher training—so that down the road you have some at your disposal to dig up and use as the situation demands.

"I don't believe in grooming hair into odd shapes—it's unnatural. Look at people in historic times. Way back, everyone had long hair, men and women, and nobody ever said it was inappropriate. Since hair will keep growing from the head, I think we should let it grow rather than interfere with its course. It's like music that floats our way. If we were to cover our ears, we wouldn't be able to discern its melody. We need to let it travel through to our brain. We have to let things follow their own course. It's the same with hair. We have to let it walk its path. Don't you think so, Lila?" He finally managed to sound pretty sharp. All that studying to get a diploma hadn't been a waste of time after all.

There was no way to tell if the girl sitting in the seat next to him had paid attention to even a sentence or two of his elaborate speech, but her stillness and silence seemed to suggest she had been thinking along in her head. When she revealed her mind, she sounded like someone who had been working her brain hard: "But come to think of it, fifty thousand's not so little. Some people have to work almost a year to save that kind of money."

"Don't sell it. I was just asking hypothetically. It's your trademark. If you sell it, your pretty face would be missing something." He smiled at her, but Lila wasn't looking his way. She was staring into space, off in another dimension, because she was still caught in her train of thought.

"But if I were going to sell it to you, would you buy it?"

Mr. Pravit glanced sideways, his gaze accidentally latching on the girl's cleavage. "Where would I get fifty thousand baht?"

Lila smiled to herself. She gradually let her legs move a little further apart as she leaned back, smooshing and spreading her hair against the backrest, making herself more comfortable.

"You don't have to pay it all in one go. You can split it into installments. Once you've paid the full fifty thousand, I'll cut my hair off and give it to you. You could maybe pay me three or four thousand at a time. We can negotiate the amount each time—just as long as it's not under two thousand."

Gripped by her proposition, Mr. Pravit could barely pay any attention to the road, to see what color the traffic lights were or whether any cars wanted to overtake. Much like the evening's encroaching darkness, some kind of mysterious power was obscuring the light in his heart. He wanted to ask Lila frankly whether he understood whatever was going on correctly. Her body language and her words, were they signaling whatever he was thinking in his head? But the teacher-in-training didn't dare open his mouth, for fear of being perceived as green—he was, after all, almost ten years older than she was.

"We're almost at your house." He went for a descriptive group of words, using a matter-of-fact tone.

"Do you want it? Do we have a deal? Are you buying it?" Lila stuck her hand out and shook him on his left thigh, shooting waves of electricity that made multiple glands in his body shiver and shake.

He nodded, feeling as if one giant bead of sweat was running down his whole body.

Lila grinned so broadly her shapely cheeks nearly burst. "Should we start today?"

He nodded and quietly gulped. "Two thousand, OK?"

There was no answer, but nor was there an objection.

"In that case, you don't have to drop me off yet.

We can go somewhere first."

The report concerning these two hair-obsessed people will end with a conversation between Pravit and his girlfriend Jai, who called the young teacher's cellphone before he turned the car down a side street that had a conspicuous sign out front reading PLERN 73 HOTEL.

"Yup. I'm going to pick up some food for my mother and swing by hers," Pravit held the phone flat against his ear.

We don't know what his girlfriend said on the line, but he answered: "I'll be there before eight for sure, I swear on my hair."

The time Pravit had decided to grow his hair long, having inspected his person to see which physical attributes he could alter or adjust to fashion himself in the image of an artist according to his imagination…

He'd forgotten…

… that he had to inspect deeper down into the heart of that image.

PART 9: EYE SPY:
A ONE-ACT PLAY

The setting is a cinema.

It doesn't need to look any particular way, as long as it has the requisite level of darkness for showing a movie. Go ahead, go nuts with the modern technologies. Blast away with a surround sound system with as many speakers as desired. The rectangular screen can be large or small, flat or curved, mounted high or low, no problem. The seats can be covered in leather, corduroy, or velvet—that doesn't matter. Likewise, how many degrees the backs can be reclined, how much the legs are confined, how tightly elbows have to be entwined, and how the cup-holders are designed— these aren't important details. As long as the place has the look of a movie theater, that suffices for the telling of the story.

The day of the incident in question is a normal day of the week—not a weekend, not the first or last day of the month, not a day with a solar eclipse, not February 14 or 29, not an actual or observed holiday, not a day with a coup d'état, not a day with an apocalyptic flood, not a Quit Smoking Day. It's an ordinary day, with most people's lives taking their usual course: those who have to clock in and work morning to evening under neon lights in air-conditioned rooms must keep persisting and suffering through. Those who have to study must keep pushing themselves almost to the point of madness. Those who have to pray must keep holding their hands joined in prayer. Those with managerial responsibilities must keep attending meetings. Those who have to sweep the streets must keep on swinging their brooms. Those who have to beg must keep their palms outstretched. Those who have to govern the country must keep up the corruption. All in all, the day is entirely normal. True, it's a bit boring, but deep down everyone's happy for the banality to be maintained, if trading it away meant sacrificing certainty and stability along with it. We, therefore, have movie theaters to serve as showrooms for excitement, variety, passion and chutzpah, with these qualities working as antidotes for the inertia inside the minds of city folks.

(The principal observation regarding the behavior of members of society as a whole: safety first.)

Monday, Tuesday, Wednesday, Thursday, Friday—
feel free to choose one of the five.

We would recommend Wednesday because it's the
most impartial, it's not pushing limits, it's not taking
sides. It gets along with everyone. Character-wise, it's
like a chameleon, changing colors as if it were nothing. Anything can happen on a Wednesday.

The time of the incident is early afternoon, somewhere between the 1:00 p.m. and 2:00 p.m. screenings,
a time when most people cannot slip away from their
primary duties to go catch a movie.

But today is a day that's slightly out of the ordinary for Namfon, a woman twenty years of age or
somewhere in that ballpark, wearing a white T-shirt
untucked over her black university-uniform skirt.
She should be sitting with a textbook open in front
of her within the four corners of a room along with
other people her age. But this morning, she was feeling rebellious and decided, randomly, to break away
from the confines of her routine by wandering around
instead, riding the bus aimlessly past the university
campus with her hand clinging to the rail. She got
off here and there until she decided to buy the paper
ticket that allowed her admission through the doors,
to come and sit in this dark room, to watch a movie
and kill a couple of hours before she resumes her rov-

ing and idling as she waits for the sun to go down.

(A commentary between the lines: Namfon's killing of time is a killing of the value of time simultaneously. But since it's time we're talking about, no matter how you kill it, it doesn't ever die. So, the time that is killed can still have value if Namfon knows how to find value from the experience that takes place during the time that is killed. Still, whether the value of the time that is lost in the cinema is worth the ticket price that she had to fork over for it, is something that has to be evaluated for life.)

When Namfon goes in and takes her seat before the movie starts, no one else is in the theater. She's the lone spectator. What movie's about to be shown, Namfon hadn't paid much attention to that fact. It happens to be showing just at the right time for her, so she'd blindly pointed to it. The reason she came in wasn't to search for truth or even art in the images that are about to prance and prowl on the screen. All she'd gleaned from the promotional poster out front was that this movie featured a man and a woman, neither of whom is too shabby-looking; they certainly aren't so hideous that she couldn't spare a couple of hours or so sitting back and looking at them. The plot likely has something to do with the pair. They either love or hate each other, either get it on or kill each other off. The ending will either be happy or sad, or maybe it will take an unexpected turn. Namfon can handle watching any of that—it can take as many turns as it wants, or it can turn so much there's nowhere else to turn, she's fine with that, too. As long as it ends, her criterion is met.

Namfon brings only herself into the theater. She's not holding a cup of soda or a bucket of popcorn in her hands.

Her seat is located in the middle. To say it's left wouldn't be right, and to say it's right wouldn't be quite. To say it's close to the screen would be a half-truth; to say it's far from the screen would be a half-lie. Let's say, she chooses a seat that's quite close to the center of the room so she has a good view of the screen and we have a good view of her as well.

At the start, when the lights first come on, they're bright enough that every seat is visible. Namfon is already settled in her seat, her face angled slightly upward. The tilt of her chin indicates that her eyes are focused on a point on the screen. (We cannot see the screen ourselves because the idea is that we're sitting where it's supposed to be, but we see glimmers of light dancing and flickering on the plane of Namfon's face—the effect is meant to help us imagine that something is being projected in front of her.)

Namfon looks blankly at the screen, not paying much attention to what is being shown. From the accompanying sounds—not very loud—it's possible to gather that what's supposedly playing on screen is in all likelihood a commercial or a preview and not yet the actual movie. In any case, the room is still too bright for a film screening.

The lights slowly dim, but the shifting eyes on Namfon's face remain as visible as before.

The royal anthem plays. Namfon looks around and doesn't see anyone in the theater besides herself.

(Note: The royal anthem is playing in the whole theater, which means we all, too, have to get up and stand at attention promptly, so Namfon appears to be the only person not standing.) But when she turns straight ahead, she jumps as she sees the entire theater of people up on their feet. She springs up from her seat immediately, looking embarrassed and ashamed for having hesitated.

The anthem ends. Everyone, including Namfon, sits down again. She appears to be getting into position to watch the movie, with her eyes on the screen and her hands neatly in her lap.

Suddenly, the lights go out in the whole theater (Namfon's, not ours).

Three seconds later, they flash on again.

The lights bring with them the figure of a man. We can tell his gender straight away from his apparel—a black button-down shirt, black slacks—as well as his build and complexion, also on the darker end of the spectrum as if to coordinate with his clothes.

More noteworthy than the other details, though, is the fact that he's wearing dark glasses, which give him an aura of mystery. We wonder why he's sitting in such a place, whether he realizes the purpose of the venue, and if he does, whether he has mental issues which might explain why he would intentionally come into a movie theater wearing sunglasses.

This mysterious gentleman is seated diagonally one row in front of Namfon. He's sitting still, not paying attention to his surroundings. At first, Namfon herself doesn't take any special interest in the sudden appearance of the man. But given that he's the only other person in the audience, our heroine is bound to notice him and develop a natural curiosity. She inches her head forward into his row, covertly examining the profile of his face. She's probably asking herself the same question we are: "Why is he wearing sunglasses?"

The music begins to fill the room, signaling that the film's about to start. Her eyes restless, Namfon goes back and forth between a glance at the screen here and a stolen side-eyed look at the mysterious man there. It's unlikely she's focused enough to be able to piece together the plot that's unveiling itself.

When she can't stand to pretend to ignore the elephant in the room any longer, Namfon leans over the backs of the seats in the row in front, on the verge of inquiring about his puzzling behavior. Since they're the only people in the entire theater, she presumes she wouldn't be annoying anyone else by striking up a conversation.

But before she's able to get a word out, the man beats her to it, his voice nearly making her heart plummet and shatter on the floor and scatter like popcorn.

Mysterious Man: Shouldn't you be at school?

For a minute, Namfon is dumbstruck. Or is he one of the professors among the many she doesn't know? Probably not, since he doesn't look at all familiar. Namfon tries to get a better look at him again, but darkness tends not to cooperate in an attempt to get an accurate picture.

Namfon: Do you know me, Mister?

Mysterious Man: Don't worry, I don't know you.

Namfon: Then how do you know that I'm supposed to be at school?

Mysterious Man: (soft laughter) I just took a stab in the dark. Am I right or not?

Namfon doesn't answer. She leans back in her seat, the expression on her face suddenly tense. She doesn't like it when someone sounds like a know-it-all. It really gets on her nerves. Namfon sits there chewing over the situation for a moment before firing up her voice again.

Namfon: What about you? What's with the sunglasses in a movie theater? Are you insane?

The man doesn't reply. He simply lets the uncomfortable mood hang in the air and diffuse like particles of dust.

Namfon can't bear the atmosphere in the room. What she's breathing in is giving her an itchy burn that she can't quite find the words to describe.

Namfon: How are you going to follow the movie like that?

Mysterious Man: If you don't zip your mouth, I probably won't be able to follow it.

Namfon thrusts herself toward the man's seat and snatches the glasses from his face so lightning-fast that anyone would probably be taken by surprise. With his glasses removed, the mysterious man swiftly ducks down, hiding his face in his palms, which are on his lap.

Namfon: Let's see what you can see with these glasses on.

Mysterious Man: (face still hidden in his palms, so his voice is muffled) Give them back now! Rascal! Don't you know what's sacred and what's profane? How can you mess with a grown-up this way?

Namfon: (wearing the sunglasses) Whooooa! It's pitch-black.

She peels the glasses off, shakes her head a few times in an attempt to shimmy the darkness out of her eye sockets. Then she glances over at the owner of the glasses: he's still holding the same sorry posture. Namfon leans toward him with her left arm out-stretched and taps him on his bowed back.

Namfon: What's wrong, Mister? You can't do without the glasses or what? Are you about to black out or something? Here, take them back. If I'd kept them on any longer, I probably would have gone blind. What weird glasses!

With her right hand, she passes the glasses back to him. The man cautiously reaches his hand out to take them, all the while taking care not to let his face lift up too far from his lap. Once the glasses are finally placed back on the bridge of his nose, he gradually unfurls himself and leans back, more at ease.

Mysterious Man: Your parents did not raise you properly.

Namfon: Hey! Leave my parents out of this.

Momentarily seized by indignation, Namfon leans in and snatches the glasses from the man's face again, and this time, as before, he immediately throws his face into his lap, covering his eyes with his palms.

Mysterious Man: You! You jerk! Give that back!

Namfon: It's your fault for being rude. This time I'm not giving them back until you tell me what's the matter with you. Why do you have to wear the dark glasses? Why can't you do without them?

With his hands still blocking his face, the man suddenly twists around and, with one hand, tries to grab his precious possession back. Namfon leans away in time. She springs up from her seat and jumps over the backrest, landing on a seat one row behind, just beyond his reach.

Mysterious Man: (shouting) Don't you dare take them! Give them back!

Namfon: First answer me: why have you come in here to watch a movie with dark glasses on?

Mysterious Man: I didn't come to watch.

Namfon: Then why did you come? Are you insane or something?

Mysterious Man: I came to listen.

His remark makes Namfon pause as she processes. He came to listen. Oh no! Is this middle-aged man blind? If that's really the case, then what she's been doing is the worst thing she's ever done in her life. She's been harassing a physically disabled person who merely wishes to participate in a normal activity like everybody else. It is such a depraved act that even the most hardened criminal would find it intolerable. What should she do? Is there a way to ask for forgiveness that would somewhat lessen the hurt and embarrassment that she unintentionally inflicted on this poor older man, as if adding another wound to his life?

Namfon quickly shuffles back to her seat, looking panicked.

Namfon: (handing the glasses back to the mysterious man) Oh no! I must get down on my hands and knees and apologize to you, sir. It really hadn't occurred to me that your eyes were impaired.

Taking the glasses from her hand, the man swiftly puts them on his face.

Mysterious Man: (smiling) My eyes aren't impaired.

What is this supposed to mean? Namfon feels fooled. She rarely finds herself having to offer anyone an apology. Her expression starts to look muddled as it morphs from one of shame to one of anger.

But the man doesn't give her an opportunity to start hurling insults.

Mysterious Man: But I have no eyes.

Namfon: (her voice shaking) What? What do you mean you have no eyes?

Mysterious Man: So you really want to know (reaching up to take his glasses by the legs)? It's like this.

Once the glasses are removed, the theater is flooded with light, revealing every surface of every prop, along with the skin below the man's eyebrows, on either side of his nose and above the apples of his cheeks.

He has holes for eyes!

Meaning: both of his eye sockets are deep cavities, devoid of anything that could conceivably be called a part of an eyeball. There aren't even lids to cover the two dark caverns.

Namfon: (covering her mouth with her hands) Ahhh! Holey-eyed ghost!

The man bursts into laughter, and with that the audience erupts, each drowning out the sound of the other. Even louder is the thunderous clapping that follows.

The curtains drop... That's the end of the show.

The applause doesn't die down, and an instant later, the curtains are raised again. Namfon and the mysterious gentleman hold hands as they come out for a bow, accepting praise from below.

As the ultimate bow for the night's performance, Namfon grabs her hair and yanks on it until her head rips off.

The audience whistles loudly in a show of delight.

It's another success for us.

But we have to admit, it's an old formula for this sort of comedy.

A play that parodies the living, who's going to be caught dead missing out on that?

PART 10: LONG HEART

BC got dust in his eyes.

Try as he did to use his left index finger to rub it out (his right hand was busy fumbling with the wallet, looking for banknotes to pay for the ride), the irritation was proving stubborn. BC had a problem with dust. Not quite enough to cause him serious health issues, but it'd been a source of aggravation for a long time—based on his age, it probably came to over a hundred and thirty years by now. His trouble with it might be traced back to the fact that he had been born into a household that conducted an antiques business. BC's first memory was of his father blowing and wiping a layer of dust off a wind-up clock. He didn't recall if in that moment he'd been sitting or standing or how far he'd been from his father, but what remained fixed in his mind was that his father's breath had transported the dust from the dial of the ancient time-teller into his, BC's, eyes.

It had stung and itched, no different from the sensation in his eyes now.

"I don't have any change, sir," the driver turned to say. Scoffing to himself, BC nodded, visibly irked, and let the driver nab all the cash from his hand.

Once he had his earnings tucked away in his pants pocket, the driver looked out, surveying the surroundings and then pausing his eyes on two utility poles that lay collapsed in shambles on the sidewalk. "This area looks dangerous. Do you know anybody around here?" he asked BC as if out of concern, although his tone was nothing but cold.

"This is my old neighborhood. I'm very familiar with it," BC responded as he pushed the door open.

"There's a phone over there." The driver stuck his right arm out the window and pointed at a rundown glass booth on the street corner ahead. BC tried to stare in that direction, but his eyes hadn't recovered. "If something seems suspicious, or if you can't find a ride back, call me. My number's on the rear windshield." His finger went with his words. "An area in neglect like this seems like it would be a hotbed for lurking hoodlums. Better be careful."

By then BC was already out of the car and standing fully upright on the road. His eyes were starting to feel less irritated. After he shut the car door, he responded to the well-meaning driver through the rolled-down window: "It's alright. If you go left along this road for not even fifteen minutes, there's a small community living there. It won't be hard to find a cab back."

"Can I ask you something?" The driver hadn't stepped on the gas pedal; the engine was humming and panting like a large animal snoring. "What are you doing here? The buildings and the houses are all demolished, there's practically no trace of what was here before, and it's been this way for thirty or forty years now."

At first BC didn't react. Then he bent down, supporting himself by holding on to the top of the driver's side window with both hands, so he and the cabbie were at eye level. The curved posture of his spine made his whole body feel stiff.

"I'm here for a visit," he said finally, and then snickered.

The driver had his eyes locked on BC's face. He began to take note of the way this large-framed man was dressed: the brown jacket that BC was wearing appeared to be genuine leather. He tried to guess BC's age from his complexion, but in this day and age, it was difficult to discern merely from external appearance the true state of someone's core. The trend among people with sufficient means was to have the capacities of their life spans adjusted by multiple units at a time. The more money they had, the greater the level of concealment—or 'preservation' (the technical term favored in reference to the process of organ supplementation)—they were able to achieve.

BC appeared to be a person of means. The neatness and the quality of his clothes, as well as his accent and the manner in which he spoke, seemed enough to suggest that he was sufficiently rich to have been through the preservation process (and by more than a few pieces at that), particularly his hearts. The driver honed in on BC's chest, trying to surmise with his eyes how many supplementary BP hearts (Beat Plus was the world's preeminent manufacturer of computer hearts) this man had had implanted (each one can add thirty units of life preservation; the latest price came to about eleven million baht apiece). But there was no way anybody could guess correctly.

Annoyed by the driver hanging back, BC straightened up and waved goodbye.

"Good luck," the driver said before pulling away, leaving a trail of opaque white smoke blowing out from the exhaust pipe. BC hung his gaze on the departing car, simply to have something to look at. He noticed that the phone number on the rear window was missing two digits, and felt a certain relief that now there was no need to clutter his brain with it.

He sauntered along the sidewalk, from time to time shielding his face from the dust. When he reached the telephone booth, he slipped in and grabbed the outmoded apparatus's bright-red receiver and put it against his right ear.

As he'd expected, the line was silent: the telephone had long been dead.

He continued along the path, his eyes noting the surroundings as he walked. Two filthy plastic trash bins lay tumbled and purposeless in the middle of the road. Everywhere he looked, waste paper and scraps of food were strewn about. The store sign of a once-popular Chinese restaurant lay fallen in a broken heap in front of an abandoned shophouse. BC peered deep into the obscurity of the structure's interior, and then stuck his tongue out to give his lips a quick lick.

There, the flavor of stewed-beef soup, recalled from memory, snuck up, notwithstanding that over a century had gone by.

"BC, BC, BC," the shrill voice of the restaurant owners' impish daughter had struck BC and his family's ears one evening. They were sitting at a round table, savoring the noodles they were bringing to their mouths with chopsticks. BC was only seven-and-a-half years old then.

"What kind of person's called BC? That's a weird name."

Although he was displeased with the girl's ill-mannered greeting, that voice made BC start to wonder about his name, despite the fact that he had never found it strange.

"What does my name mean, Mom?" Putting his chopsticks down (he was not very skilled with them yet), BC turned to interrogate his mother, who was chomping on Chinese broccoli next to him.

"Ask your father. He named you." His mother steered the tip of her chin in the direction of his father, who was sipping tea with a smile.

"B and C are English letters, short for 'before Christ,' meaning the era before Jesus Christ," his father keenly explained, "which I took for its connotation of ancientness, of antiquity. When an object dates back to a B.C. era, that means it's very old, that it has great archeological value."

New vocabulary was being dumped into the boy's little brain. He didn't understand his father's explanation, but he nodded along obligingly, in the manner that he had observed adults do while they conversed.

Then BC turned to his mother again: "Who's

Jesus Christ?"

"Why don't you ask your father? He knows better than I do." Her chin motioned a direction once again.

"Jesus Christ is the prophet of one of the world religions called Christianity," replied the expert, who then ate a bite of noodles from his chopsticks. "It's a faith with many followers."

Faith, prophet, followers. His head was spinning. There were many things in the world he didn't understand, his own name being one of them. "And am I a follower of the faith?" As far as the boy was concerned, faith and fun could have approximately the same meaning. His only impression was that it seemed a good course of action; otherwise so many people wouldn't be doing it, as his father had just told him they did.

"No, no, we're Buddhists," his father chuckled. "That means we follow and worship Buddha, not Jesus." He paused for a breather, taking one gulp of his tea. "The reason I named you BC is just because it conveys an era that is long bygone, because I like antiques, because we have an antique shop, that's all."

BC remembered how he didn't used to like telling his classmates that his home was an antique store, even though it was a business that generated a decent amount of income for his family; it ought not to have been anything embarrassing. But the word "antiques"—kong gao—literally means "old things," and it didn't sit well with BC. Despite his father's telling him how the older things are, the more valuable they become, BC imagined antiques as objects past their useful lives, so rundown and dated they were repulsive, things he didn't like touching his skin. He would have preferred shiny, brand-new things he could show off to his friends. Contemporary toys were what he wanted to possess. Over the head of his bed hung an antique clock of his father's. It was a grand object that produced a nice sound; it ticked powerfully. But as a boy, BC had wanted a compact digital clock that flashed red, or else an alarm clock with cartoon characters like the ones his friends all had. He never wanted to invite friends over to play because he didn't want them to see the panoply of hideous objects that were strewn about in nearly every corner of his house.

Because he was taken with new objects and modern inventions, BC grew up to be an electrical engineer, one endowed with precise hands and an imaginative mind. His timing was opportune as the fields of replacement organ research and human parts product design were booming. Before he'd even graduated, BC held the reputable post of department supervisor for research and development, oversee-ing the latest advances in parts at the Part Human Research Company.

The Asian headquarters of PHR's parent company was a splashy, glaring glass dome in the Central District of Hong Kong Island where BC had lived for almost ten years, until he was lured away to work with a small research team in Tokyo called Beat Plus Corporation. At the time, the company had just started to focus on creating a full-circuit computer the size of a fist, which would be able to replace the human heart per-fectly in every aspect of its functionality. Moreover, it would be able to add life and slow the aging process by upward of a hundred years. When BC reported to work the first day, that was still a mere dream and tar-get for the organization.

Only fifteen years later, that dream had come to fruition and at a level beyond satisfaction.

Overnight, Beat Plus Corporation (BPC) became a name bearing prestige, and with that it acquired one of the strongest business negotiation positions on earth. Takaeshi Kosuki, the company's owner, was instantly transformed from a mad mind into a world-class billionaire. Because of his product, in the present day, our world had many, many people over a hundred years old walking about, blending in society without anyone being able to pick them out easily, unless those people had previously been famous and known to the public. Hundreds of leaders who had influenced world politics and the global economy going back six decades were all still alive and in the same form as before (that is, if they hadn't been killed in an accident or by a noxious disease earlier), certainly without any change that would be noticeable at a glimpse.

The first BP heart implant could prolong life by about thirty years. If more was desired, a user had to buy an additional program. Each one cost the same as the first; there was no discount. If a user wanted sixty units of life-preservation in one go, the price was twenty-two million baht. If ninety units, it would be eleven million more and so on.

Nobody knew what BPC's technology could achieve in terms of the maximum capability of its product, but there was no doubt that with the thirty life-unit hearts, they were holding back solely for commercial reasons. Even though the company publicly communicated that setting the preservation level at thirty years was shown in tests to be the most balanced result, in tune with the natural workings of the systems of the human body, and posing a zero-percent risk (there had been only two customers who had experienced minor side effects from the use of BPs), multiple sources confirmed that one BP should very easily be able to add fifty units of life-preservation.

Regarding this point, BC, one of the people in the know, had declined to comment.

He realized full well that he'd taken part in the coup against nature, which for a while, back when he was forty-one, had been a sensation, and since he was the only Thai on BPC's pioneering team, the name BC made an even bigger splash all over the country.

After he had celebrated his one hundred-and-twenty-fifth birthday (with the appearance of a forty-two-year-old man), BC clinked glasses to bid farewell to his position as one of the top executives of the company, and returned to settle down in a private beachside villa in Hua Hin, although he still served as a consultant for several of the world's large enterprises.

Five years ago, BC's name had returned to the limelight again when Naowei announced that he had participated in the design of the Blink Cam, the latest development in image recording.

Users only needed to have an operation to insert a special film into the lens of either eye and link a hair-thin wire to neurons somewhere in their bodies, and they would be able to record any memory they could see with their eyes. The images were stored as waves that ran through the wire as floating data. When users wanted to enjoy the pictures (capturing the birth of their first child, for example), they had only to close their eyes and think of what they wanted to see, and the memory waves would display on demand brightly colored images on the inside of their eyelids for their personal viewing.

"Dreams come true, all the time," was the Blink Cam's tagline.

Personally, BC didn't particularly marvel at this piece of work. He viewed it merely as an expensive toy without any real use. He helped with its design and creation to amuse himself—it beat sitting around looking at the waves in the ocean, day in, day out.

The BP heart was not capable of preventing death.

It could not protect people from unforeseen natural disasters, could not reverse an accident or a homicide. What it did was preserve the lives of the fortunate, allowing them to continue humming along for an extended period.

It was an invention that remained under the dominion of destruction.

If you hit it with a hammer, it would smash into pieces.

It wasn't god.

Without additional programs, its efficacy would dwindle and its useful life would eventually expire.

Like his father's antique clock.

Like this little street that used to be full of life.

BC's feet came to a stop in front of a store with a glass front, which no longer had a single pane of glass intact. All the panels had cracks and multiple bits broken off, and their surfaces were covered in thick layers of mud and dust.

He pushed the front door in with his foot, creating enough of a gap for him to squeeze himself through. As dust sprinkled onto his head like rain, he shielded his face with his hand.

—

"Are you sure you recognized him?" The long-haired guy in the backseat leaned his face over the taxi driver's left shoulder. "You're sure the guy was really BC? Don't you bring us to a godforsaken place like this just to grab at water."

"I'm pretty sure." Cigarette balancing between his lips, the driver sped to the corner and then hooked a left, cocking his wrists to turn the steering wheel. "That face, no wonder the whole way I thought he looked familiar somehow."

"What's a guy like him doing around here? It's so

freakin' dirty. Even I don't want to come here," the man with long hair said as he looked out, inspecting the area.

"He said it was his old neighborhood or something like that," the driver said, cigarette smoke swirling out of his mouth but swiftly dissipating when swept by a breeze. "Maybe he misses the past."

In the backseat next to the guy with long hair, another man sat looking severe. His face was obscured to the world by the shadow of the brim of his woven cowboy hat, which rendered the hardened look in his eyes impossible to detect.

"Just let it be true," The long-haired man grinned with guile. "In an abandoned area like this, it's easy to do anything. There's not even a dog around to witness a thing," he said, and then he nudged Cowboy's side with his left elbow. "Hey, how many units do you think he's got left?"

Cowboy's mouth started to move but even as words came out, the rest of his face didn't stir. "Someone at that level, I guarantee it's a ton."

His partner laughed, satisfied. He then clapped the driver on the shoulder.

"Hey, if it's really him, and we get the job done, you'll get a bigger cut." His cheeks got hit with a blast of hot air from outside. "Because this time the take-home's going to be who knows how many times more massive than usual."

Although Cowboy didn't voice an opinion, when his right hand felt the outline of the knife handle that protruded from inside his jacket pocket, his chin bobbed up and down, encapsulating his sentiment.

—

Inside the place that used to be the antique shop, BC was standing in front of a cupboard. Once upon a time, it used to be polished to shiny perfection every day to augment the luster and the allure of the silver displayed on the shelves behind the glass.

Everyone in the family had died in a fire back when he was toiling away designing the heart for BPC in Tokyo.

Everyone had become the past; they had become antiques.

BC had dedicated his life to work. He never had a family of his own and never wanted to have one.

Antiques aren't objects of value, no, BC thought as he used his palm to wipe a layer of dust off the cupboard so that the flesh of the wood could come up for air. Normally, he didn't like even to look at dust particles.

Antiques aren't objects of value because only their

outer shells remain; their essence has long vanished. Their values lie only in grimy memories that can't be concretely measured.

Are memories enough for people?

BC shook his head.

A clock that can no longer tell time has no use, of course, but what I helped build, it boosts the quality of life; it gives someone like me the opportunity to invent new things, to continue helping to develop the world for hundreds of years longer. If I let nature take its course and allow myself to grow old, I would be left with a rundown body, depleted in its potency. I would be able to live on only as trash, until my last breath.

To this day, BC continued to believe in newness.

Dust wafted into his nostrils.

He sneezed.

—

"Somewhere around here, for sure," the driver turned to tell the two men in the backseat. The car was now parked next to the signal-less telephone booth.

"Let's go. Let's get our asses out and do some gutting." The long-haired guy kicked the door out with the heel of his leather shoe.

Cowboy coolly flipped the door handle, got out

and stretched on the street. Then he took his hat off and dusted it couple of times.

"First we've got to wai the bastard and call him grandpa—his heart's lasted over a hundred years! That's a long time!" his partner said as he reached into his pocket for his weapon.

Cowboy cracked a smile so slight it was nearly imperceptible.

"But life, in reality, is short for everybody."

PART 11: BUTT PLUG

Paan put his right hand over his mouth in an attempt to conceal that it was wide open.

How many times had he yawned that morning, he'd stopped counting, but he found this last one the most satisfying because it brought air all the way down to the bottom of his heart.

Not many actions managed to approach that area.

This yawn of his contained not a pinch of drowsiness or exhaustion; it consisted purely of tedium.

Tedium, be it from life or work, tended to be able to drag his mood down like no other feeling.

"Sigh": that was the sound of self-pity that followed.

"Sigh," Paan lamented to himself. "When am I going to be dead?"

And then he got up from his chair and stepped toward the window, holding in his right fist a white eraser that he rolled as a little distraction, like a die.

Each side of the gummy cube, smooth and squishy, had been written on in Paan's own hand, which was somewhat sloppy. One side said "doomed," another one said "doomed," another one said "doomed," another one said "doomed," another one said "doomed," and the last said "doomed."

Standing in front of the rectangular window looking out on some portion of the city, Paan shook his fist awhile and then opened his hand, letting the eraser tumble and bounce on the floor.

As there was no need to check what he'd rolled, Paan mumbled, "Doomed again, me, forever doomed," without shifting his eyes to verify.

He peered through the window at the building across the way, but he wasn't looking at anything in particular, because in truth his eyes were staring inward, digging for some meaning within himself. Paan was pondering again (how many times had he done this in his life, he'd lost count) where his true self was.

He was zoned out, but deeply and with purpose.

Then suddenly something unusual flashed in front of his eyes.

A naked human body had fallen past the window and down onto the street. It happened so quickly Paan nearly couldn't tell what it was. But without a doubt the nearly unidentifiable object had arms and legs, which enabled him to come up, in time, with the hypothesis that it was a human body.

Shocked, he nearly planted his face against the glass as he rolled his eyes diagonally downward, following the trajectory of the obscene body.

Since the building he was in wasn't as tall as the horizon, Paan had no trouble discerning what had just plunged down onto the concrete. The blood spreading from the region of the head was washed over by sunlight, which made it gleam conspicuously. Paan touched the glass with raised hands, as if the move would bring him closer to the corpse.

Did he know the deceased? If the person had jumped from this building, it was probably someone from among the crowd whose face he must have seen and whose eyes he must have met many times. Perhaps they had even relieved themselves standing next to each other, or else perhaps they had shared a table at the cafeteria.

While he was weighing whether to go down and look at the deceased's face so as not to have to wonder anymore, Paan suddenly noticed the normality of everything that surrounded the naked body lying in a pool of blood.

It was the most suspicious normality that he had

ever witnessed.

Not one person was paying attention to this death.

It was absolutely impossible that no one had picked up on it yet. It wasn't as if the body was tiny, like a little bird. On top of that, the body had not a shred of clothing clinging to it. The thick red liquid fanning out profusely from the corpse couldn't exactly pass for a puddle of gasoline commonly seen on roadways. Why didn't a single head turn and look? Why didn't a single vehicle care to slow down or park and investigate? Was he the only witness privy to the naked suicide below?

Paan couldn't very well bear the curiosity any longer. Swiftly turning away from the window, he looked beyond the glass wall of his office at the crew of employees who had to put up with letting him call them his underlings. No matter on whom his eyes landed, that individual's focus was firmly fixed on his or her task, as if glued to it. Each person's attention meandered only within a small radius around him or her. Nobody met his gaze; nobody communicated with him through body language. Paan realized then that if he were to strip completely naked and step over the windowsill into the air, casting himself down like that man on the street, without first sending out a warning, not a soul would notice.

But he wasn't ready to do that. He might be fed up to death, but the tedium he suffered was largely limited to the professional sphere of his life, mostly contained in the room with the eraser that constantly reminded him of his doomed fortune.

Paan pushed the door open and let himself out. He wanted to announce to everyone the news of what had unfolded before his eyes, but he held back, wanting to wait until he saw the deceased's face so he could give a more detailed report. Thus he hurried to the silver-doored elevator located before the corner with the toilets and, jabbing his finger, called it down from the twentieth floor to come pick him up.

When the elevator arrived, parting its doors open to let him in, Paan entered to find two female office workers standing close together in a way that suggested they were friends who had been debating a life issue of some sort just before he intruded in on them. He glanced at the two of them only briefly, but the feeling that a mood had been interrupted was palpable. One of the two women was clutching a handkerchief in her left hand. The other had her right hand on her friend's side, a posture that was almost a comforting embrace, but Paan didn't detect a single drop of tear that would provide concrete proof of some kind of sadness.

Or did the woman with the handkerchief have something to do with the naked man on the street?

The G button was already illuminated on the floor-button panel; all three of them were headed to the same level.

"A moment ago," Paan spoke up after a ceremonious cough. As anticipated, his voice held the attention of both pairs of eyes. "I was looking out the window in my office, and suddenly I saw a person's body plunging to the ground." Paan paused to assess the reaction on the listeners' faces, picking up only a look in their eyes urging him to continue with the story. "It was a man's body, and he wasn't wearing any clothes. He smashed hard onto the street—there's no way he survived. His body's still lying there right now, drowned in a pool of blood. I'm about to go see if it's somebody who worked in this building with us."

With the four eyes belonging to the two listeners lingering on his face, Paan was surprised to find that the two women appeared wholly unaffected by the story, given its disturbing content.

"The two of you probably hadn't heard about it?"

The woman fisting the handkerchief slowly shook her head. The tails of her eyebrows sloped downward, giving her face an instant appearance of sorrow. But the other woman was the one who spoke up: "Why would we have already heard about it?" she asked, her voice packed with distrust.

"I just figured... " Paan was stumbling. "I thought..." He was struggling to find the appropriate explanation. "I feared that you two... " All the effort was making him feel massively uneasy in the chest. "I'd considered it possible... "

The two ladies were still waiting for one complete sentence.

Pann took a deep breath and said, "My guess was that you two were venting to each other or comforting each other about something, given the ambiance in here when I walked in, so in my mind I'd linked it to the naked man who'd just jumped off the side of the building and died right before my eyes, and I thought it was possible that there was a connection. But if I misconstrued things, please accept my apologies. I didn't mean to offend you." Paan averted his eyes and hung his gaze on the panel of buttons instead; he was growing impatient with the slowness of the elevator today.

"Next time don't presume you can draw whatever conclusions you want with other people's business. It's inappropriate and ill-advised." This time her voice was gentler than before, giving Paan a small amount of mental relief. "What you'd guessed—that my friend and I had been comforting each other before you got into the elevator—that's true." Her friend nodded. "But it doesn't have anything to do with anyone jumping off the side of a building."

Paan was already set to say, yes, I understand now, never mind, I apologize again. But before he could rattle off something along those lines, the woman cut in and picked up with her story, leaving him no window of opportunity to end the conversation.

"I'm sorry if what I'm about to say doesn't sound too nice, but I believe that the problem that my friend here is going through in her life is much, much more dire and cruel than somebody's death, because my friend is still alive and has to endure this horrible misery. People who are already dead are rid of any worries, right? But how much longer my friend will have to go on suffering, that can't be predicted."

Paan listened with great interest: such an arrangement of words touched him on a personal level. He himself had been left so down and depressed by problems before, to the point that he had felt death was in fact something positive, not something to be mourned over in the least. But before he could get too carried away commiserating along with the voice that was almost quivering, the elevator signaled that it had brought the passengers safely to their destination.

"I'm a manager on the twelfth floor. If there's anything I can do to help... " Paan managed to say that much before the elevator doors separated, "... I would be happy to."

Without coordinating their responses, both women smiled just at the corners of their mouths, but the talkative one added, "Thank you, and I apologize for raising my voice a little unreasonably earlier. I happened to be wrapped up in an emotional moment with my friend."

"It's alright. Don't worry about it." As the three were already standing in front of the elevator, five other people wedged themselves through their conversation in an attempt to spring for the door, which was already closing.

"Would you be able to tell me in broad terms what's troubling you? In case I can try and come up with a way to help in the meantime," Paan purposely looked straight at the woman to whom the problem belonged, who had kept mum the entire time. He wanted to hear the sorrow in her voice so that he could be sure he hadn't been emotionally played for a fool.

"I... " She finally unsealed her lips, letting the words trickle out: "My butt plug is no longer functioning, that's what the doctor says."

From every syllable he'd heard, Paan felt certain that this woman's distress defied words in its enormity. He didn't know how he could keep looking her in the face without showing obvious pity. The tediousness of his own life began to fade from his mind: in the face of someone with a deteriorated butt plug, who could possibly have the heart to agonize over trivial problems of his own?

"I'm really sorry to hear that."

"Yes, I'm really sorry, too." On the unlucky woman's face, a faint smile still dared to pop up. "But don't concern yourself—now you know probably nothing will be able to help me. I have to learn on my own to live life without a butt plug. Thanks for asking."

Several minutes after the two women had already said goodbye, walked off and disappeared around a corner, Paan was still standing there stunned. He wanted to help the woman, but since the world hadn't been able to find a way to treat a deteriorated butt plug, he didn't see how his fumbling for a solution could lead anywhere.

His throat felt parched. Probably, the fluid that normally kept that area moist had been diverted by the body to another part currently in need of hydration and care.

If he could get a few gulps of pure water into his

stomach, it might make him feel better, Paan told himself.

He started walking but his steps were sluggish because his brain still refused to focus its energy fully on the legs.

As he exited the building through the glass doors, out of the corner of his eye, he spotted a store he knew.

They sell water there, he thought.

Paan began crossing the street, fixated on the idea that the refreshing sensation would help wash away the gloom.

He hadn't made his way through traffic and onto the other sidewalk yet when his right leg stumbled on something that nearly made him fall.

But because of his superior balance he regained his footing and walked on.

The only thing he thought was:

Streets these days…

… are so full of clutter.

This edition published in the United Kingdom by Tilted Axis Press in 2018. This translation was funded by Arts Council England.

tiltedaxispress.com

First published in Thai by Guy Marut Press as ส่วนที่เคลื่อนไหว (*Suan Ti Kleunwai*) in Bangkok in 2001.

ISBN (paperback)   9781911284185
ISBN (ebook)   9781911284178

A catalogue record for this book is available from the British Library.

Edited by Saba Ahmed
Cover design by Soraya Gilanni Viljoen
Typesetting and ebook production by Simon Collinson
Printed and bound by Clays Ltd, Elcograf S.p.A.

This book has been selected to receive financial assistance from English PEN's "PEN Translates" programme.

Supported using public funding by
**ARTS COUNCIL
ENGLAND**

ABOUT TILTED AXIS PRESS

Founded in 2015 and based in Sheffield and London, Tilted Axis is a not-for-profit press on a mission to shake up contemporary international literature.

Tilted Axis publishes the books that might not otherwise make it into English, for the very reasons that make them exciting to us – artistic originality, radical vision, the sense that here is something new.

Tilting the axis of world literature from the centre to the margins allows us to challenge that very division. These margins are spaces of compelling innovation, where multiple traditions spark new forms and translation plays a crucial role.

As part of carving out a new direction in the publishing industry, Tilted Axis is also dedicated to improving access. We're proud to pay our translators the proper rate, and to operate without unpaid interns.

We hope you find this fantastic book as thrilling and beguiling as we do, and if you do, we'd love to know.

tiltedaxispress.com

@TiltedAxisPress